MURDER
AFTER
MIDNIGHT

BY GREG FOWLKES

MURDER AFTER MIDNIGHT

© 2018 The Fictional Press
www.TheFictionalPress.com

The Fictional Press is a small, independent press specializing in the publication of fictional works by emerging authors. If you are interested in bringing your fictional works to life in print as well as electronically, contact us! We can help!

www.TheFictionalPress.com

ISBN 13: 978-1-943403-47-9

Printed in the United States of America

Books by Greg Fowlkes

From the Wizard at Law Series:
The Laws of Magic
Trial by Magic

From the Murder on Mars Series:
Blood Red Sands of Mars
A Death at Station Alpha
A Corpse in Hut Town
Murder at the Mars Club

From the Fictional Detective Series:
The Fictional Detective
A Fictional Detective Trifecta

Star City Stories: Space Opera Noir Featuring Frank Sladek

The Uncorrupted Corpse

Tequila Visions

Cargo From Paradise

Ice Viking

1.

This story starts out the way that every good detective story, the kinds that are printed on cheap paper, starts. It ends the way that every good detective story ends too, which is badly. But that's for later.

I was sitting in my office late one afternoon. Unusually for San Francisco, even in August, it was hot and humid. The window was open, and the electric fan sitting on top of the filing cabinet was pushing the warm, muggy air around ineffectually, but I was still sweating. There was a bottle of cheap rye standing on the scarred top of the desk and a squat tumbler half full of amber liquid sat next to it. The glass could have used some ice, but I didn't have any.

The black lettering on the glass of the office door that read "Tolliver Detective Agency" makes it sound like a big operation, but the reality is that there is just me, Jim Tolliver. I don't have a receptionist, not that there would have been much for one to do. Business had been down of late. The agency did have an answering service, at least in those months I was able to pay the bill.

Maybe that's why she came in person, knocking on the glass of the door to the outer office. I got up to see who was there. I could see her silhouette backlit by the dirty white globe that hung from the ceiling in the hallway; I could tell it was a woman by the curves in the shadow on the glass. I straightened my tie, hid the glass and bottle, then went and opened the door.

She was tall for a woman and slender, but as I've just mentioned, not so slender that she didn't have curves in all the right places. She had shoulder length brown hair that verged on auburn pulled back on her neck. In the dim light, I couldn't tell the color of her eyes, but I would have guessed that they were green. She was wearing a black silk dress, the kind of dress that wealthy widows wear when mourning recently dead husbands.

"Won't you come in? I assume you *are* here for the detective agency."

"Yes, I am. Are you Mr. Tolliver?" Her voice matched her figure, a little low for a woman's voice, but smooth and round in all the right places. It was a refined voice as well. Her care with her diction and enunciation spoke of a proper education, or of someone pretending to one.

"Yes, I am. James Tolliver at your service. Why don't you come in and have a seat and tell me what we can do for you." As I've explained I work alone; I used the "we" in the editorial sense. There was only "me," and I intended to give this client my personal attention.

"Thank you, Mr. Tolliver."

She allowed me to escort her to one of the chairs facing the desk. She had the good manners not to inspect it first to see if it was dusty. Either that or she just didn't care.

After she was seated, she said, "My name is Helen Mauston. I wish to hire you to look into the death of my husband, Charles Mauston." Straight to the point. I liked that. Most women, and most men, for that matter have trouble coming to the point when they hire a private detective, as if there was something shameful about it. Of course, there often is.

"Is there a reason that you want his death investigated, Mrs. Mauston?"

"Yes. I believe that my husband was murdered, Mr. Tolliver. I want you to find the person responsible."

"You have to understand, Mrs. Mauston, that murder is a matter for the police. They don't take kindly to outside interference."

"But that's just the trouble, Mr. Tolliver. The police don't believe that my husband *was* murdered. They consider his death to have been a suicide and have closed the case. That's why I need a private detective."

I looked at Mrs. Mauston from across the desk, trying to get a read on her. She looked to be in her early thirties but could have been a few years younger or older. I couldn't see her hands because she was wearing black gloves. You can tell a lot about a person from their hands. Perhaps later I'd get a look at hers. For the moment I'd have to judge her by what I could see, and what I could see was a woman who was used to getting her own way.

"Is there any particular reason why you believe that your husband was murdered, Mrs. Mauston?"

"Charles wasn't the kind of person who would kill himself, Mr. Tolliver. Not without a good reason. My husband was what they call 'a self-made man.' He'd come up the hard way, mostly in the Orient, and was not the kind of man to run away from anything. But to answer your question, Mr. Tolliver, no, I don't have any particular evidence that would indicate my husband was murdered. I just believe that it was highly unlikely."

"I take it Mr. Mauston was wealthy—"

"Wealthy enough, Mr. Tolliver. He was a partner in an import/export business, a reasonably profitable one. If you are worried about whether I am able to pay your fee—"

I interrupted, "That's not it at all, Mrs. Mauston, though we can discuss that later. My point is this, the police take the death of wealthy men seriously, more seriously than they would, oh, say, a drunken sailor or a Chinaman. If there were any indication that your husband's death was anything other than a suicide, they would have followed that up. If they didn't find anything, chances are I won't either. I wouldn't want to take the case under false pretenses, Mrs. Mauston."

"I'm sorry, Mr. Tolliver. I didn't mean to be rude—" She had, of course, but I could live with that. "It's just that it is very important to me to prove that my husband was murdered and that his death was not a suicide."

I studied her face. I'd been right; her eyes *were* green. There was a fire in them, too, the kind of fire a man could come to like, provided he didn't get burned. There was ice in them, as well, but that was something I'd discover later.

"There's something you're not telling me, Mrs. Mauston. Something you're leaving out."

"I might as well be honest with you, Mr. Tolliver. When we were married, my husband took out an insurance policy on his life, a quite substantial policy. Unfortunately, the policy contains a clause that eliminates any payout in the case of a suicide. As things stand, the insurance company is refusing to pay out. That's another reason why I don't believe my husband committed suicide. He would have known that if he killed himself, I wouldn't be able to collect on the policy."

"I see, Mrs. Mauston. Out of curiosity, just how large a policy are we talking about?"

"Two hundred and fifty thousand dollars."

"Two hundred fifty G's. That's a lot of money. Certainly enough money to provide a motive for murder. Are you sure you didn't bump off your husband yourself, Mrs. Mauston?" I said it as a jest, but I was interested in seeing her reaction as well.

She started to rise. "I can see that I've come to the wrong place, Mr. Tolliver."

"I'm sorry, Mrs. Mauston. You'll have to excuse me. I'm afraid my mouth sometimes gets carried away with itself. It has a tendency to get me into trouble."

For the first time since she had appeared at my door a hint of a smile crossed her face. She lowered herself back into the chair.

"Tell me, Mr. Tolliver, would I have come to a detective if I had killed my husband? After the police had ruled Charles's death a suicide?"

"A good point, Mrs. Mauston. Unless you thought I could prove his death a murder, but not prove that you were the murderer. Or *wouldn't* prove you the murderer. Two hundred and fifty thousand might be worth the risk."

"Still, you have to admit, Mr. Tolliver, that it would be taking a big risk."

I could see that this line of conversation was getting us nowhere. Mrs. Mauston was at least as smart as I was, as well as being better looking.

"Let's assume for the moment that you didn't kill your husband. What can you tell me about his death?"

"What do you want to know, Mr. Tolliver?"

"The details. As an example, when was he killed?"

"Three weeks ago. August second, or more correctly, the third. The medical examiner placed the time of death at a little after midnight, though I understand these things are inexact."

"They're usually close enough. And where did this happen?"

"At his office. His company maintains a warehouse and salesroom down near the waterfront. The offices were on the second floor. Charles often worked there late. He was found by the office manager when he came in the next morning."

"And just why did the police decide it was a suicide?"

"Charles was found slumped over his desk. There was a pistol lying next to him, the one that killed him. There also was a note—Do I have to go all over this, Mr. Tolliver? Can't you get this information from the police report or whatever?" Her voice rose with this. If she was faking hysterics, she was doing a good job of it.

"I could, and I probably will, Mrs. Mauston, but I'd rather hear it from you first. After all, you were closest to your husband. You might recognize the significance of something that the police would miss."

She seemed to pull herself together. "Yes, of course."

"You mentioned a note—"

"Yes. The police showed it to me. It was in Charles' handwriting. It read 'I intend to put an end to this—' I'm afraid that was all it said. It appeared to be unfinished."

"Was it signed?"

"No—As I said, it was unfinished."

"That's kind of unusual. People who leave notes when they commit suicide usually finish them. After all, they aren't going to get a chance to do so later. They usually sign them, too."

"Are you always this heartless, Mr. Tolliver?"

"I'm afraid it comes with the territory, Mrs. Mauston."

"You're right, though. That's one of the reasons I don't believe it was a suicide."

"But the police did?"

"There was the note and the gun. There were no signs of a struggle. The office hadn't been broken into. I guess I can't blame the police for reaching the conclusion that they did, I just don't believe that it was the right one."

"And you have two-hundred and fifty thousand reasons to think otherwise."

"That's not why I came to you, Mr. Tolliver. I want justice for my husband."

"Of course." If she was faking the outrage, she was a decent actress. "Getting back to the circumstances of your husband's death. Was the pistol found on his desk his?"

"No, it wasn't."

"Do you happen to know what kind of gun it was?"

"As a matter of fact, I do. It was an automatic. A .25 caliber."

"That's kind of a small gun for a man, Mrs. Mauston. More of a ladies gun, the kind that can be slipped in a handbag. Are you're sure that it wasn't your husband's?"

"Yes, Mr. Tolliver. I'm sure. You see, it was mine."

"You don't say."

"Yes. Charles bought it for me just after we were married. For protection."

"Any idea how it ended up at your husband's office?"

"No, Mr. Tolliver. I dislike guns. I never carried it. When Charles gave it to me, I stuck it in a drawer and left it there. I hadn't seen it in months. I can only assume that Charles had taken it for reasons of his own."

"And the police are sure that it was *that* gun that killed your husband?"

"So they said."

"Frankly, Mrs. Mauston, I'm a little surprised that the police were so quick to rule it a suicide, seeing as your husband was killed with your gun and the insurance policy and all. The police know about the insurance?"

"Yes, they do, Mr. Tolliver. I didn't try to conceal its existence from them. In fact, I suspect that it was pressure from the insurance company that resulted in their ruling the death a suicide."

"Understandable, seeing as it saved them from having to pay out two-hundred and fifty grand."

"Does everything come down to money with you, Mr. Tolliver?"

"Usually. I find money is at the root of most things I deal with."

"You've asked a lot of questions, Mr. Tolliver, but you haven't said whether you will take the case."

"Oh, I'll take the case, Mrs. Mauston. Provided you can pay me. My rates are a fifty dollars a day plus expenses. I'll provide an itemized bill for those. I usually require an advance. A check is acceptable, but cash is preferred."

"I had expected something of that sort, Mr. Tolliver." She reached into her handbag and pulled out an envelope. "There is five hundred dollars inside. That should be enough to cover the first week. We can make further arrangements if your investigation takes longer."

I opened the flap of the envelope. There were five crisp C-notes that looked like they had come straight from a bank.

"That will do nicely, Mrs. Mauston. Fortunately, I'm free at the moment and can get right to work on your case." That got a rise of her eyebrow and the hint of a smile. "Is there anything else you wish to tell me?"

"No, I don't believe so."

"And you've no idea who might have killed your husband? Any enemies that you know of?"

"No. Charles wasn't a quarrelsome man, Mr. Tolliver. In fact, he was rather boring. At one time I thought differently, but—"

"But?"

"You have to understand, Mr. Tolliver, I met Charles on a ship coming back from Honolulu. I thought him rather dashing at the time, though he was older than me. He would tell these stories of his adventures in the Orient. They made him sound quite the adventurer."

"But the reality was different?" I prompted.

"Oh, don't get me wrong, Mr. Tolliver. I have no reason to believe that the stories weren't true. It's just that, at heart, my husband was basically just a businessman."

"Do you think that his murder might have had anything to do with his time in the Far East?"

"I don't know. I suppose that might be it, Mr. Tolliver. Something in his past. Something to do with China, probably. I can't think of any other reason for anyone to have killed Charles."

She sounded pretty vague for someone with so much at stake.

"But you don't know of any specific threat? Something your husband might have mentioned?"

"No, Mr. Tolliver. I think I've told you all I know."

Either that, I thought, or all she was going to.

"It's not a lot to go on, Mrs. Mauston, but I've started cases with less."

"Here's my card if you need to get in touch with me." She reached into her handbag and handed me a visiting card listing her address and phone number.

"I'll let you know as soon as I turn up anything."

She rose then, and I escorted her to the door. I stood in the doorway watching as she walked towards the elevator. It was a sight worth looking at.

2.

At the time, I wasn't quite sure what to make of Mrs. Mauston. Despite the near hysterics, she had seemed, overall, a pretty cool character, the kind that just might bump off her husband if she had a good enough reason to, and I had to admit that two hundred and fifty grand made a pretty good reason. Of course, it was just possible that she really had loved her husband, and that she really was motivated by the need for justice. Anything was possible. After all, she *had* married her husband. One thing was clear though; I had five crisp, new C-notes sitting in my wallet that I hadn't had half an hour earlier, and I might as well start earning them.

I'd read about Mauston's death in the papers at the time, but I hadn't paid much attention to the details. It was time to refresh my memories. I stuffed my hat on my head and headed out. After spending the afternoon in a stuffy office, I needed some fresh air, so I decided to walk. It wasn't that far, and the exercise would do me good. As I walked down Larkin towards the library, there was a hint of a breeze off the bay that almost made it pleasant. A lot of other people must have felt the same way because the sidewalks were crowded with pedestrians headed no place in particular.

Libraries are a wonderful thing, and the public library of a major city is one of a detective's best friends. You can find information on just about anything if you take the time to learn your way around the place. Besides, it's warm and dry when it's cold and wet outside, and a great place to hang around when you aren't flush with cash. Grab a book or a newspaper and a chair in the reading room, and you can go for hours without having anyone hassling you. Needless to say, I was a card-carrying member.

I fetched the papers for the week Mauston had died and found an unoccupied table in the reading room where I could spread them out.

The accounts in the papers pretty much told the same story as that which Mrs. Mauston had related to me. The evening edition of the *Chronicle* on the third had a short notice in the local section under the headline "Local Businessman Found Shot," and went on to describe how the body had been found by the office manager, Thomas Nilgren, shortly after he had arrived at work that morning. There weren't a lot of details, except for the fact that Mauston had been shot.

In the next day's edition, the accounts were lengthier, which was to be expected. The story had moved to the second page with the heading:

Businessman Found Dead
Police Suspect Suicide

There was a file photo of Mauston looking businesslike and professional and another of his partner who was younger and slicker looking. Next to them was a photo of Mrs. Mauston looking like anything but a grieving widow. I guessed that the paper had included it on the theory that you can never go wrong by printing a picture of a good looking woman. The police hadn't released many more details, so the article was padded out with background information on Mauston and his business, mostly chamber of commerce sort of stuff. His company, Far Eastern Specialties, had, at least according to the paper, been a successful enterprise dealing with imports mainly from China, French Indo-China, Siam, and Malaya, though also Australia and some of the Pacific islands. The firm dealt in antiques, native handicrafts, and artwork from the region, mostly geared towards interior decorators looking for something "unique and authentic." The article implied that there was nothing about the nature of the business indicating a motive for suicide.

Details of his past were a bit more sketchy, but according to the paper Charles Mauston had gone out to the Orient as a young man, arriving just in time to get caught up in the Boxer Rebellion. Having survived that experience, he had remained in the Orient for the next several decades traveling from Hong Kong to

Singapore and back living what the reporter termed a "colorful" existence, though exactly what that entailed wasn't made clear. Mauston seemed to have been involved in a series of endeavors of a mostly legitimate nature. It was during the period immediately after the end of the war that Mauston appeared to have made his fortune. The article claimed that there were unsubstantiated rumors that he had somehow profited from the collapse of Russia and the stream of aristocratic refugees that had streamed through Shanghai.

He had returned to the States in the early 20's to establish the firm Far Eastern Specialties and been living in San Francisco as a respectable businessman ever since. It didn't appear that he'd been particularly active in the city's social scene, though that had changed briefly after his marriage. If he had been involved in charitable causes, he hadn't sought publicity for it. Charles Mauston, at least according to the paper, remained something of an enigma.

The next day's story gave more of the grizzly details of the death including the medical examiner's findings and a description of the gun and crime scene. Again, the account in the paper followed reasonably closely to that which Mrs. Mauston had related to me.

What I did find curious were some of the things that she had left out during our conversation. The most obvious thing was that Charles Mauston had been 55 while the paper gave Mrs. Mauston's age as 32, something of which I had no reason to doubt. Now I'm sure many marriages with such an age difference are quite happy, but when you have an older man and a much younger woman, there is bound to be speculation, especially when the man ends up dead. Perhaps just as curious was why Mrs. Mauston had failed to mention to me that Mauston had had a partner, Edward Lomax, whose age the paper gave as 37. Had there been something going on between him and Mrs. Mauston? Was that why she hadn't mentioned Lomax to me? Of course, it might mean nothing. According to the paper, Lomax had been out of town on business at the time of Mauston's death. If so, he certainly had a better alibi than Mrs. Mauston.

By the next day's editions, the papers had dropped the story. Evidently, there hadn't been enough of either gory details or scandal to be worth reporting on.

Out of curiosity, I went back to the desk and asked for the papers from the week after the date that had been given for the marriage of the Maustons. I didn't expect that the event had been considered news, but I was interested in seeing what the society page had had to say. You can learn a lot from the society section of a paper if you know how to read between the lines. I found the notice of the nuptials posted the day after the wedding. It hadn't been a church wedding but instead had been a civil ceremony at the courthouse presided over by a municipal court judge. There was a photo of the couple above the article. Mrs. Mauston looked fetching in a well-tailored suit with a big smile on her puss. Mr. Mauston looked, well, respectable and prosperous which might have explained his wife's smile.

The notice was a little sketchy on the bride's antecedents. Usually, they will at least say something like "the daughter of Mrs. and Mrs. Smith of Mill Creek, Michigan," but all the paper said was that she was "lately of Honolulu, Hawaii where she had worked as an entertainer." The type of entertainment wasn't specified. I hadn't been aware that Honolulu was a major theatrical center, but then what did I know? The implication, at least, was that Mrs. Mauston might have been something of a gold-digger. Not that there is anything wrong with digging gold. After all, California had been built on it. It did make me wonder exactly what type of woman my client was, though I think I had a pretty good idea.

I returned the papers to the desk and left the building. Outside, in the plaza in front of the library, I found a bench where I could sit and think. My trip to the library, while informative, hadn't really given me a handle on the case, but then if all the answers could be found in libraries, people wouldn't need detectives, would they? By that time it was early evening, and I debated whether to find a drink or dinner. In the end, I did neither.

One tidbit of information I had gleaned from the newspapers was that the police investigator who had been assigned to the case was Detective Lt. Albert Miller. I wasn't exactly friends with the sergeant, but we got along okay, as long as neither of us pushed the other too far. He was, by current standards, a reasonably honest cop and there was just a chance that if there was something that the police hadn't divulged to the press, he might let it slip to me.

I made my way to the Hall of Justice, on the off chance that Miller would be in. It was an even bet, as Homicide detectives tended to work odd hours. My luck must have been with me because I found Miller at his desk.

Miller is a big German from some small burg east of the Mississippi. He's got thinning hair, is a few inches over six feet, and more than a few pounds over two hundred, but a lot of that is muscle. His story is that he came west as a young man just before the war. He couldn't find honest work, so he became a cop. His size had allowed him to bang heads together when he was walking a beat, and the fact that he had a few brains in his head had led to a promotion to detective. He didn't play politics, so he wasn't going to go any further, but that seemed to be all right with him.

When he looked up and saw my face, I could tell he wasn't any too happy to see me, but I took the hard wooden chair next to his desk anyway.

He greeted me with, "What's a two-bit shamus doing amongst honest folk?"

"I could ask you the same thing, Al, but I won't."

I thought he was going to make a snappy reply, but he must have thought it wasn't worth the bother. "I assume you're here for more than just making my life miserable. What do you want, Tolliver?"

"I read that you're working the Mauston case?"

"Was working. The case is closed. I wrote my report and passed it on to the D. A. What's your interest?"

"I've been hired by the widow."

He looked up at me with just a hint of surprise. "Oh? What's her angle?"

"She wants me to prove that it was murder. Something about an insurance policy." I figured that there wasn't any harm in spilling the latter. If Miller had done any kind of a job, he probably knew all about it. The widow had admitted as much.

"I'm afraid the widow is out of luck. Pretty clear case of suicide. Mauston was found with a pistol next to him on his desk. He'd been alone in the office. There was no sign of a struggle. The pistol had belonged to his wife, but Mauston could have got his hands on it anytime. No reason to think anyone else was involved. The D. A. agrees."

"Yeah, I read all that in the papers. It's just that the widow has paid me, and I need to do my job. I don't suppose you'd let me see the police report?"

"You know I can't do that, Tolliver. It's against policy."

"Yeah. I know. But there's no policy against your reading it while I sit here quiet as a church mouse, is there? If you should move your lips or say the words out loud while you read it, I won't tell anyone."

Miller looked like he was going to refuse, but then he must have decided he'd get rid of me quicker if he just gave in. Sometimes being annoying works better than trying to put pressure on someone. I'm good at either one.

He reached into one of the drawers of his desk and pulled out a manila folder. It wasn't very thick, but then it probably didn't need to be.

"Any part in particular that you want me not to show you?"

"You can skip the M.E.'s report and the ballistics unless there's something that wasn't in the papers. I'll take it as a given that he's dead and that the pistol did it. I'm more interested in the other players."

"Not much there," Miller replied. He read me the notes that had been taken of the interviews with Nilgren the office manager and Mrs. Mauston, but it was all stuff that I already knew. Mrs. Mauston had been upfront about the insurance policy, but then she had probably known that it would come out anyway. The interview with the partner, Lomax, was more informative because the papers had pretty much ignored him as he'd been out of town at the time.

"How about this Lomax character? Did you check up on his alibi?"

"Don't insult my intelligence, Tolliver. Of course we did. He was out of town on business. Chicago until the 30th of July, then he went to Denver for a day before continuing on to Salt Lake City. We confirmed the hotels that he stayed in and some of the appointments he made. It all checked out."

"Younger woman like Mrs. Mauston, an older husband, the younger partner—Is he good looking, this Lomax character?"

"Yeah, if you like that type. Which I don't." The sneer in Miller's voice indicated that his opinion of the partner pretty much matched the one I had formed from the picture in the paper.

"I never thought you did."

"Don't crack wise with me, Tolliver. I'm not in the mood. And not after I've been giving you inside information."

"Sorry. My mouth runs away with me sometimes."

"Maybe there's something going on between those two, maybe not, but it doesn't matter because he was in Salt Lake City at the time Mauston killed himself."

"Is that the line you're sticking to?"

"It's what I wrote in my report. It happens to be what I think, too."

"Okay. Let's forget Lomax. The papers said that Mauston died right after midnight. Is that right?"

"Give or take," Miller answered with a shrug. "The M.E. didn't see the body until eight or nine hours later, so he wouldn't pin himself down, but a cleaning lady comes in at ten each night to tidy up. She said she left around eleven-thirty and Mauston was still alive when she did, so just after midnight seems a good bet. She said he was alone in the office and that she locked up after herself when she left."

Miller seemed satisfied with the fact that the death had occurred just after midnight. I didn't see any reason to doubt him, so I changed to another line of thought. "Mauston didn't have any enemies, did he? According to the papers, he seems to have had a colorful past."

"The papers say a lot of things, mostly because they look good in print. If Mauston had any enemies, no one brought them up when we interviewed them. There weren't any prints in Mauston's office that didn't belong there, either."

"Who's prints *were* there."

"Mauston's, the office manager's, those of the secretary. There were some old ones of Lomax and the wife, too, but nothing that seemed like it was from the day he died. Like I said, as far as we can tell, Mauston was alone when he died. It was suicide, Tolliver, and I dare you to make it something else."

"Too bad for the widow, I guess."

"Yeah, too bad. I feel for her, but somehow I think Mrs. Mauston will manage. Dames like that always do."

"Just what do you mean by that?"

"You've talked with her. Judge for yourself. Now get out of here. I want to go home."

Miller can be obstinate when he feels like it, so I got.

3.

In the morning, I looked up the address of Far Eastern Specialties in the city directory. It was a couple of blocks up from the waterfront just to the north of Telegraph Hill. With the five hundred bucks from Mrs. Mauston, I was feeling flush enough to take a cab, but instead, I took a cable car down to the wharf with the intention of walking up to the offices to get the lay of the land. There was a cool breeze coming off the bay, and it was early enough that the heat hadn't built up yet.

The block that housed Far Eastern consisted mostly of small warehouses facing the bay. On the other side of the block were a row of offices and storefronts, some of which were attached to the warehouses, and some of which were just free standing. The address of Far Eastern was in the middle of the block where I found a doorway set back into a shallow niche flanked by two storefronts. The name of the firm was painted on the glass of the door in black block letters. The glass wasn't particularly clean, but I could see a narrow staircase leading up to the second floor.

I tried the latch of the door, but it was locked. Evidently, Far Eastern Specialties didn't encourage casual visitors. There was a doorbell next to the door with a small sign reading "ring for service." I was about to push the button when I thought better of it and stepped back to examine the building.

The storefront to one side seemed to be the booking office of a small steamship company, the kind that could arrange passage on a freighter to places like Bora-Bora or Santiago, Chile. There were some faded posters of "exotic" locales taped to the window, and I could see a bored looking fellow sitting at a desk reading a newspaper.

It was the storefront on the other side that caught my attention, though. This had a collection of oriental artifacts displayed in the window. I don't know much about things like that, but these looked like the real deal, much more authentic than what you find a few blocks away in Chinatown. There was an impressive looking bronze urn about eighteen inches high decorated with Chinese characters and covered with the kind of green patina that is hard to fake, along with a brass figure of the Buddha and some smaller pieces carved from a greenish rock that I took to be jade. What had caught my eye, though was the name of the shop. Painted on the glass in gold leaf was the name "Far Eastern Specialties" done up in the kind of fake lettering that is supposed to look like Chinese. I remembered from the newspaper accounts that Mauston's firm dealt in antiquities and artwork and realized that the store must be connected with the business. On a hunch, I decided to check it out.

Unlike the shops in Chinatown, the store seemed to operate on the theory of quality rather than quantity. There were a number of well-lit display cases and stands that looked more like a museum or art gallery than a tourist trap. Other items were hung on the wall. Much of it was Chinese, but quite a few pieces I judged to be Malaysian or Indian in origin. Next, to each item, there was a neatly lettered card with a description and a price. Nothing seemed to be cheap.

As with the stuff in the window, everything looked authentic and expensive, but what caught my eye was the woman standing behind a counter that held small jade items. If this were one of those detective stories I referred to earlier, she would have been wearing a tight-fitting sleeveless dress of red silk embroidered with dragons or something, her shining black hair arranged in some elaborate Chinese hairstyle and she would have studied me with an inscrutable oriental gaze.

Instead, she was dressed rather primly in a white silk blouse and a straight charcoal gray skirt, her hair was pulled back on her neck in a simple bun, and she was watching me with a curiosity that could hardly be termed inscrutable. Though tall for an oriental, and on the slender side, there were still enough curves to make it clear that she was a woman. She was looking at me through almond eyes, alright, but there was a hint of a smile on her lips as if at some private joke.

I turned away and pretended to study a case filled with oriental weaponry.

"Are you interested in swords, Mr.—?"

Her voice matched her complexion, smooth and slightly dusky. There was also a hint of an accent, not so much Chinese as French.

"Tolliver. Jim Tolliver. And no, I'm not particularly interested in swords. I find that they're a little hard to hide underneath a trench coat."

She chuckled at that, a real laugh, not a tea-house giggle.

"Ah, I see you are a practical man, Mr. Tolliver. I'm afraid this may not be the shop for you. As you can see, we mostly deal in the extravagant, not the practical. But beautiful, nonetheless if you know what you're looking at."

She seemed to be studying me as if I were one of the artifacts wondering if she knew what she was looking at.

"I'm always up for appreciating the beautiful, Miss—"

"Bouchet, Florence Bouchet." She must have seen something in my face for she added, "And to answer your question, Mr. Tolliver, my father was French. He met my mother while working as a manager on a rubber plantation. I was born in Saigon."

"I didn't mean to pry, Miss Bouchet," I said, trying to flash my most endearing smile.

She looked at me for a second before giving a hint of a smile. "Why do I doubt that Mr. Tolliver? I get the feeling that you rather make a habit of prying."

"I guess I'm just a curious fellow, Miss Bouchet."

"They say curiosity killed the cat, Mr. Tolliver."

"Good thing I'm not a cat, then. It hasn't killed me yet."

She didn't seem to know how to respond to that. Either that, or she was growing tired of the banter.

"Was there anything in particular that you were interested in? In addition to what is on display in the showroom, we have any number of items in the warehouse if you are looking for something specific."

"Oh, I wasn't looking for anything in particular. I was just curious. Someone I know mentioned the store in passing. I was in the neighborhood, so I thought I'd drop in and have a look."

"Who was your friend? Perhaps I know them."

"It was Mrs. Mauston, actually. I believe that her husband was one of the owners."

A curious expression crossed her face at the mention of Mrs. Mauston. I gathered that she didn't quite approve of the owner's wife.

"You are a friend of Mrs. Mauston?"

"No. Ours is more of a business relationship."

She raised one of her exquisitely shaped eye-brows.

"I'm afraid I've presented myself under false pretenses. I'm a private investigator, Miss Bouchet.   I've been hired by Mrs. Mauston to look into the death of her husband. Did you know Mr. Mauston well?"

"No. Not really, Mr. Tolliver. He didn't have much to do with the day to day running of the shop. That is handled by myself and Mr. Li, the manager.   Of course, I would see him around occasionally, but we didn't work together closely."

"I see. And the other partner, Mr. Lomax, do you work with him?"

"On occasion.   He mostly handles outside sales and acquisitions. He travels a great deal, so no, I don't know him well either."

"You've been most helpful, Miss Bouchet."

"Tell me, Mr. Tolliver, do you have some reason to think that Mr. Mauston's death has anything to do with this shop?"

"No. I don't know what to think, yet. I was just hired by Mrs. Mauston yesterday, and I'm still trying to figure things out."

"If there is anything I can do to help, Mr. Tolliver—" She went to the counter and picked up a business card from a stack there. "Here's my card. It has my home telephone number as well. If you think of anything else that you'd like to ask me, feel free."   I couldn't tell whether she meant that in more general terms or not.

"I'll keep that in mind, Miss Bouchet. I'll get out of your hair now. I really came down here to see the business offices. They're upstairs, aren't they?"

"Yes, but there's no need for you to go back out to the street. There's a way to reach them through the warehouse. If you'll just give me a moment to call ahead and make sure it's alright."

She went back behind the counter where there was a phone. There must have been a direct line to the office because she was connected immediately. There was a short conversation and then she hung up.

"You can go right on up, Mr. Tolliver. Mr. Nilgren is expecting you. It's right through this door. There's a stairway on the left. Take that, and there is a door at the top that opens into the office."

"Thank you, again, Miss Bouchet. You've been a big help."

As I took the indicated door, I could feel her gaze on my back. I wasn't quite sure what was on Miss Bouchet's mind, but it occurred to me that it might be interesting to find out.

After going through the door, I found myself in what was a typical warehouse space, a large, poorly lit, high ceilinged room with crates stacked in more or less orderly rows. Many of the boxes were stenciled in different oriental languages in addition to English. From their size and shape, it was hard to judge what the contents might be. They certainly could be art objects and oriental artifacts. They could just have easily held machine guns and hand grenades—or farming implements. But I wasn't concerned with the boxes. As far as I knew, Far Eastern had been a legitimate business, and the contents of the crates weren't relevant to Mauston's death.

The stairway was just where Miss Bouchet had described it, a plain wooden affair, sturdy enough, but without ornament. I headed up it to the plain door at the top, which, as promised, was unlocked.

On the other side, I found myself in a largish room lit by windows facing the street. A half-dozen desks were arranged in the middle of the room while the walls were occupied by the usual filing cabinets, bookshelves, and other office equipment. There was a Chinese girl pounding away at a typewriter at one of the desks and a couple of non-oriental men sorting papers at others.

I was greeted by a short, thin man who looked to be in his mid-forties. He had thinning sandy hair, and wire-rimmed glasses with thick lenses were perched on a nondescript nose. The conservatively cut gray suit he wore looked as if he'd bought it off the rack a few years earlier. Curiously, in contrast to the rest of his outfit, he wore a brightly painted tie depicting a palm tree.

"Mr. Tolliver, I take it?"

"That's me," I said, trying to sound friendly and cheerful.

"I'm Thomas Nilgren, the office manager. What can I do for you, Mr. Tolliver? Miss Bouchet said something about you being a detective." Nilgren didn't sound either friendly or cheerful. He certainly wasn't happy to see me.

"Yes. I'm a private investigator. I've been hired by Mrs. Mauston to look into the death of her husband."

"I see," Nilgren said. I got the impression that, like Miss Bouchet, he wasn't terribly fond of Mrs. Mauston. "Well, I've already talked to the police."

"I know. But as I said, I'm a *private* investigator. I'm not associated with the police. They don't necessarily share all their information with me, so I've come to get the facts from the horse's mouth, as it were."

"And you say you're working for Mrs. Mauston? I hadn't been told anything about that."

"We could call her if you like to confirm the fact."

Nilgren looked as if he'd prefer to do anything but that.

"That won't be necessary. I suppose that it doesn't matter. I've certainly nothing to hide. Just what is it that you wish to know, Mr. Tolliver?"

"I understand that you were the one to find the body?"

The Chinese girl had stopped her typing to insert a new sheet of paper in her machine, though she seemed more interested in what we were saying than her typing.

"Yes. Unfortunately. It was most distressing. But I'm usually the first one here in the morning, to open up the office, so it was only natural that I'd be the one—"

"And what time was this?"

"I arrived just before nine o'clock as usual. I saw that the door to Mr. Mauston's office was open, so I went in to see if he was in. That's when I found him. He was slumped over his desk. At first, I thought that he had had a heart attack or stroke or something, but then I saw—"

Remembering seemed to distress Mr. Nilgren.

"You saw the blood?"

"Yes. I checked for a pulse, but of course, Mr. Mauston was quite dead. Had been dead for some hours they say."

"They being the police?"

"Yes."

"Did you see anything else? Anything out of place?"

"There was a pistol. Lying on the desk next to his hand."

"Which way was it pointing?"

"Excuse me?"

"Which way was the barrel of the gun pointing? Which way was the grip? Towards Mauston's hand or away from it?"

Nilgren looked confused for a moment and hesitated. "The barrel was pointing towards the front of the desk, and the handle was pointing away from him I think. Why? Is it important?"

"Probably not. Did you recognize the gun? Was it something Mauston kept in his office?"

"I wouldn't know, Mr. Tolliver, but I wasn't aware of Mr. Mauston keeping a weapon of any sort here at the office."

"When was the last time you saw Mauston alive?"

"The previous evening, right before I left work. That would have been at six. He was still in his office working. I stopped in to say 'good-night.' He said that he was going to meet someone for dinner and then probably come back to the office afterward to look over some papers."

"He didn't mention who he was going to have dinner with?"

"No. He didn't say."

"Was it unusual for Mauston to work late?"

"No. He did that quite often. Usually several times a week."

"So you didn't see anything out of the ordinary about it?"

"No, on the contrary, it seemed quite normal."

"What about his mood? Did he seem happy, sad, *suicidal?*"

"No. Nothing like that. Mr. Mauston wasn't the sort of person to show his feelings, at least to someone like me."

"Meaning the help?"

"If you want to put it that way. I've worked for Mr. Mauston for nearly ten years, but we never had what you'd call a personal relationship."

"What about the business? Were there any problems there that might have led Mauston to kill himself?"

Up to then, Nilgren had been answering my question, probably hoping to get rid of me as quickly as possible, but with that last one I'd crossed the line, and he'd decided to clam up.

"I'm afraid that I'm not at liberty to discuss such matters, Mr. Tolliver. If you want any information about the business, you'll have to take it up with Mr. Lomax."

I didn't see any point in pushing it with Nilgren, particularly as I might want to get some answers later. "I understand, Mr. Nilgren. In your position, I'd probably do the same. Is Mr. Lomax in?"

Nilgren looked relieved.

"Yes, I believe he is. Would you like me to ask if he will see you?"

"If you would."

Nilgren disappeared behind a door that opened off the main room. He was gone for a couple of minutes. When he came out all he said was, "Mr. Lomax will see you now," and pointed at the door.

Just before I knocked on the door, I winked at the Chinese typist. She winked back.

4.

For some reason, I took an instant dislike to Edward Lomax. I do that with some people for no good reason, but I usually find out later that I am right.

Lomax was about my height and build and probably about my age, too, in his late thirties. He had the kind of "Latin-lover" good looks and olive complexion that were all the rage with women who spent too much time at the moving pictures. Lomax knew it, too, and acted and dressed the part to the hilt down to the tailored light flannel suit, slicked back dark hair, and one of those pencil-thin mustaches that are favored by dance-hall gigolos.

As I entered his office, he got up from behind his desk and approached me, hand extended.

"Mr. Tolliver? Helen told me that she'd hired a private detective. I'm at your service, though I'm not sure what help I can be. I was out of town at the time, but then you probably knew that already."

I noted that it was "Helen" and not "Mrs. Mauston," but did that mean anything? I got the impression that Lomax was on a first name basis with lots of women, whether they reciprocated or not.

"Thank you for seeing me, Mr. Lomax," I responded in my best insurance salesman voice.

"Not at all. Please have a seat."

He directed me to a comfortable leather armchair facing his desk.

As I waited for Lomax to resume his seat behind the desk, I took a quick look around. There was a large window behind the desk. With the sun coming in it cast a sort of halo around Lomax that made him hard to look at. The rest of the office had been furnished tastefully if not extravagantly in mahogany and brown leather. The walls held a display of oriental art, mostly Japanese prints. As I'm no expert in such things, I couldn't tell whether Lomax was a connoisseur or if the display was there just for the effect.

"Just what is it you wish to know, Mr. Tolliver?"

"To tell the truth, I'm not exactly sure. Mrs. Mauston just hired me yesterday, and I'm still trying to get my bearings. Maybe the best place to start would be to ask you if you think Mr. Mauston was the kind of man that would kill himself?"

"I wouldn't have thought so. Charles wasn't what you'd call a weak man. He'd built this business from the ground up, mostly working out in the Orient, back at a time when it was a lot rougher than it is today—"

"From what I hear, it's still pretty rough."

"Not like it was twenty years ago, before the war. The locals still ran things in many places back then, and the Europeans were all trying to cut each other out. Charles never talked about it much, but from what I understand he'd gotten himself into and out of more than one tight spot. I guess what I'm trying to say, Mr. Tolliver, is that Charles Mauston wasn't the kind of man to give up easily. That's why I find it hard to believe that he would kill himself."

"What about money worries? Did Mauston have any financial problems?"

"Not as far as I was aware. Charles was careful with his money, not tight, exactly, but he wasn't one to take a lot of risks financially."

"I take it the business is doing okay."

"As well as can be expected given the shape the world is in. We still manage to pay our bills and make a decent profit. There's plenty of money to be made in the Orient if you know what you're doing, and Charles certainly knew what he was doing."

"What's going to happen now? Now that Mauston's dead?"

"I imagine we'll carry on pretty much as we've been doing. We have an established network of suppliers that the firm has done business with for years. Relationships that Charles built up when he was out there. That won't change, at least in the short term. In the long term—well, all things come to an end, eventually."

"You seem to be taking things philosophically, Mr. Lomax."

"Perhaps dealing with Orientals as much as I have, I've acquired some of their fatalism."

"If you don't mind my asking, what happens to the business with Mauston gone? Does Mrs. Mauston inherit his share of the partnership?"

"No, as a matter of fact, she doesn't. There was a survivorship clause in the papers setting up the partnership stating that if one of the partners should die, the other would assume complete ownership of all of the firm's assets and liabilities. Such clauses are not at all unusual is closely held business such as Far Eastern."

"Kind of harsh for Mrs. Mauston, isn't it?"

"Oh, it's not as bleak as you might imagine, Mr. Tolliver. All of Charles's personal holdings will still go to Helen. And then, of course, there is the insurance policy. Most people would consider a quarter of a million to be a generous provision."

"Yes, the insurance policy. Of course, Mrs. Mauston won't get that if Mr. Mauston's death is ruled a suicide."

"That's where you come in, Mr. Tolliver, isn't it? You're getting paid to prove that Charles didn't kill himself."

"I like to think I'm getting paid to find the truth."

"I'm sure you do. But I think we'd all like to make sure that Helen gets that insurance settlement."

"I'll certainly do what I can."

"I have every confidence in you, Mr. Tolliver. But the insurance policy is another reason that I don't think Charles killed himself. He would have been well aware that by doing so his wife would forfeit the insurance. I'm sure that he wouldn't have wanted that."

I didn't bring up that fact that that only applied if Mauston had still been in love with his wife.

"Just how were the relations between Mr. and Mrs. Mauston?"

"I'm not sure what you mean, Mr. Tolliver."

"I would have thought it an obvious question. There was quite a difference in their ages. Mrs. Mauston is quite attractive, and, from what I saw when she hired me, quite a spirited woman.

An older gentleman might have trouble keeping a woman like that satisfied."

"I'm not sure I like what you are implying, Mr. Tolliver."

"I'm not implying anything, Mr. Lomax, I'm just asking a question. Did the two of them get along?"

Lomax hesitated a moment as if weighing exactly what he wanted to say.

"They got along well enough, as far as I know. Probably as well as most married couples. Charles knew what he was getting into when he married Helen, and he wasn't one of those men who try to keep their wives on a short leash. As far as I know, their marriage was a happy one. Charles provided Helen with security, social standing, and an ample allowance, and from what I saw, she was content with that."

Lomax seemed to be using the phrase "as far as I know" a lot. It made me wonder if it was just a figure of speech with him or if he was trying to cover something up.

"Look, Mr. Lomax. I don't want to get off on the wrong foot here. It's my job to ask questions, and sometimes those questions can be taken the wrong way. I don't want that. Let's change the subject. I understand that you were out of town the night Mauston died?"

"Yes. I was on a business trip out east, Chicago, St. Louis, Denver. I was visiting customers, art dealers, interior decorators, and such. I make a trip like that every few months. That was my role in the partnership. Charles saw to the importation end, and I handled the sales and distribution."

"I see. Just how did the two of you become partners, anyhow? If you don't mind my asking?"

"Not at all. It was quite simple, actually. I had an interest in Oriental art, had studied it in college. I had made several trips to the Far East. That's where I met Charles, in Singapore. We got to talking one night. He was looking to expand his business, but he needed an infusion of capital. I had inherited some money, and I was getting tired of just knocking aimlessly about the world. You might not think it, Mr. Tolliver, but it was a natural fit. When we got back to the States, we had a partnership agreement drawn up. It was an equitable arrangement. Things worked out reasonably well. I don't think Charles had any regrets. I know I don't."

"Was this before or after the Mauston's were married?"

"Before, actually. Does it matter?"

"Probably not. If, as you believe, Mr. Mauston didn't kill himself, then someone must have murdered him. You've got an alibi, and I assume we can rule out Mrs. Mauston. Did Mr. Mauston have any enemies? I wouldn't have suspected the antiquities business would be that cutthroat."

"You'd be surprised, Mr. Tolliver. But as far as I know, Charles hadn't any enemies. Far Eastern has always prided itself on dealing fairly with both our suppliers and our customers."

"What about the staff? That Mr. Nilgren, for instance?"

"Thomas? I can't see it. He's treated well and paid decently. Besides, he's not the type for murder."

"In my experience, there really isn't a murderer type."

"No? Well, you'd know that better than me. But I can't see any of the firm's employees wanting Charles dead."

"If it wasn't one of your employees, what about something else related to the business. Mauston hadn't gotten himself on the wrong side of the ILA by any chance, had he?" Labor unrest had roiled the docks in recent years, and sometimes things had gotten pretty rough.

"Not to my knowledge," Lomax replied. "You have to understand that Far Eastern is a pretty small fish. We bring in a crate here, a couple of crates there. I doubt if the Longshoreman's Association even knows we exist."

I guess I wasn't really surprised. I was still trying to find an angle on the case, but the business didn't look like it. I decided to change the direction of my questions.

"What about his personal life? Did he have any enemies there?"

"I'm not sure that Charles really had a personal life, Mr. Tolliver. Not in the sense you mean, at least. He wasn't given to gambling, and as far as I know, he didn't keep a woman on the side. He didn't have any vices that I know of. He didn't dabble in politics—"

"I get the picture. What about something from his past? From what I read in the papers and what you've said, before the war he led, shall we say, an exciting life."

"I'm afraid I can't help you much there. As I said, Charles never talked about those days much. Oh, he had plenty of stories, mostly amusing, but then I think any white man who was in the Orient in those days has those. But as to real death-defying adventures, well, I tend to think that his reputation in that regard had gotten somewhat exaggerated. Not that Charles tried to discourage it, mind you. His reputation as an adventurer was good for business."

"Still, Mrs. Mauston hinted at the possibility that her husband's death might have had something to do with his past."

"Did she?" Lomax responded. He sounded surprised. "As far as I know there wasn't anything like that." He paused, then continued, "Though there was an odd incident once. Charles and I were walking to lunch, and this man accosted us on the sidewalk, He started shouting something in Russian. I don't understand the language, and all I got out of it was the word Shanghai. Odd kind of fellow, shabbily dressed, but he carried himself like a count. Charles said something back in Russian and handed the man a few dollars. He went away after that."

"Do you think that this Russian might have held enough of a grudge to have killed Mauston?"

"No, I don't think so. I got the impression he was just some kind of crank down on his luck. Charles was in Shanghai after the war; I know that much. A lot of the old Russian nobility passed through there, those that escaped the Bolsheviks, most of them with not much more than the shirts on their backs. Charles probably knew him from back then."

It wasn't much to build a murder case on.

"Okay. Let's try another angle. Far Eastern imports a lot of antiquities and art objects, many of which I assume are of a religious nature. Is it possible that something that was imported rubbed someone the wrong way?"

"You mean something like a secret Chinese criminal society or a group of assassin Tibetan monks?"

"Well, I wouldn't put it in exactly those terms, Mr. Lomax, but, yeah, something like that."

"If you think that, I'm afraid that you've been reading too much Sax Rohmer, Mr. Tolliver. Those sorts of things only exist between the covers of books or in the movies. We've never had any problems of that sort. And, as far as I know, Charles hadn't received any threatening letters or had a mysterious symbol painted in blood on his office door, either."

"So you think the notion—"

"I think you can dismiss that idea completely as a schoolboy fantasy," Lomax said with a chuckle that grated on me.

"Yeah. It does sound kind of silly, doesn't it? But, all the same, someone did kill Mauston—"

"There's no chance it was an accident?" Lomax interrupted. I wasn't sure if he was deliberately trying to change the subject or if we'd reached a dead end.

"Not from the police reports." I'd thought about that angle myself, but it hadn't seemed likely. Mauston hadn't been cleaning the weapon, and I couldn't imagine him just fooling around with it, either. He'd known how to handle firearms, and given the angle of the wound, it couldn't have been a mistake.

It was my turn to change the subject.

"Look, and I'm not trying to imply anything on her part, but is it possible that someone wanted Mauston dead because of Mrs. Mauston? Some secret admirer or someone from her past?"

"I'm afraid that you'll have to ask Helen that question. But, no, as far as I know, there's nothing in her past or personal life that could provide a motive for murder."

"So there's nothing else you can think of that might shed some light on Mauston's death?"

"I can't think of anything, Mr. Tolliver."

"Well, I've taken up enough of your time, Mr. Lomax. I'd like to thank you for answering a lot of fool questions."

"Not at all, Mr. Tolliver. Anything I can do to help Helen out."

Lomax got up from behind his desk and held out his hand. There wasn't much I could do but shake it and leave.

"Oh, there is one more thing before I go. I'd like to see Mr. Mauston's office if that would be alright?"

"I don't see why not," Lomax replied. "The police have done all they are going to in there. It's been cleaned up since—" He almost sounded embarrassed by the thought of Mauston's death. Not exactly the reaction of a man trying to hide something. "I'm not sure what you'll find in the way of clues."

"I understand. I just want to get the lay of the land, as it were."

He pressed a button on his desk, and a moment later Nilgren appeared.

"Mr. Tolliver would like to examine Mr. Mauston's office, Thomas."

The office Nilgren led me to was in the opposite front corner from Lomax's. The office manager produced a key from his pocket and unlocked the door.

"We've kept it locked since the police finished."

When I didn't comment, he pushed the door open. I walked past him into the office. He stood in the doorway a moment, unsure of what he should do, and then shut the door leaving me alone in the office.

The general layout was a mirror image of Lomax's office. The paneling was the same as in the other office, but in place of the Japanese prints, there were English hunting scenes of the sort that businessmen hang on their office walls to show they mean business. It was almost as if Mauston had been trying to separate himself from his past history in the East. The only oriental artifact in sight was a large bronze Buddha that sat on a cabinet against the side wall. It was a curious touch in a room so determinedly western.

You can tell a lot about a man from his desk. Mauston's was neat and uncluttered. Of course, it had been cleaned up, but somehow I doubted that it had looked much different while he was alive. There were the usual desk accouterments, a blotter, a pen stand with a bottle of ink, and a pair of wooden trays. They weren't labeled as such, but it was clear that one was for in and the other for out. At the moment, they were empty. A picture of Mrs. Mauston in a silver frame stood at a corner of the desk.

The desk wasn't locked, but I didn't find much of interest in the drawers, just the normal sort of papers and directories one would expect to find. The drawer over the kneehole held an assortment of pens and pencils and paperclips. There was also a stack of business cards that Mauston must have picked up over the years.

Predictably, these had been arranged in alphabetical order. As I leafed through the pile, there was nothing that struck me as being out of the ordinary except for one.

The card was for Lance Donavan. I knew the name. Donavan was a private investigator who specialized mostly in divorce work. It might mean something, or it might mean nothing, but maybe things hadn't been as good between Mr. and Mrs. Mauston as Lomax had claimed. I slipped the card into my pocket and closed the drawer.

There didn't seem much point in my sticking around. On the way out I winked at the typist again. She giggled. Nilgren shot her a dirty look but said nothing.

I left down the stairs and through the front door. Out on the street, I thought about what I'd found out, which wasn't much. Mauston hadn't had enemies, money problems, or problems with his wife. "As far as" Lomax knew, that was. If I believed him. I'd taken an instant dislike to him, and despite of, or maybe because of, his slick manner, nothing in our conversation had changed my opinion of him. But did I have any reason to doubt him outside of that annoying mustache of his?

5.

Lomax had rejected the idea that Mauston's murder had had anything to do with the Chinese side of the business, but I wasn't completely convinced. Frankly, I was grasping at straws, and I wanted a second opinion before I discarded that line of investigation. Fortunately, it was a nice day, and as I was close to Chinatown, I took a walk uphill.

Sam Sing owns a store on the border of Chinatown, the kind of shop that mostly sells cheap trinkets to tourists and sailors; paper dragons, brass plates, that kind of thing. Some of the junk probably even comes from China, though it's just as likely to have been made in Japan or even Cleveland. I knew Sam because I'd done some work for the Chinese Businessmen's Association once and he'd been the one that had hired me. I wouldn't say that we were friends exactly, but there was a certain amount of mutual respect between us that was nearly as good.

When I entered the shop, his eyes lit up, and he greeted me with a bow. He was dressed for the part in an embroidered silk jacket and wide silk pants with a little round silk hat perched on his head, but he was clean shaven and didn't sport a pigtail. The costume was all a pose for the tourists. I knew for a fact that he changed into a suit before he went home.

"Mister Jim, long time no see."

"How you doing, Sam?"

"Business is low-see, but Sam doing OK."

"I think you can drop the pidgin, Sam. It's just you and me."

Sam made a show of looking around. Sam's ancestors came over to build the railroad, and when he wants to his American is as good as mine is. Maybe better.

"I guess you're right, Jim. You still trying to make a living as a private gumshoe?"

"Yeah. You still trying to con the tourists with this junk?" I waved my hand around the crowded shop.

"It pays the rent," Sam answered.

"How's Sam Junior?"

"He's fine. He graduated from high school this year. He'll be going to college in the fall if they'll take a Chinese."

"Give him my congratulations, Sam."

"So what brings you to Chinatown? Incense, dragon kite, maybe a cleaver?"

"I'm in the market for information, Sam."

"I don't see that listed on the window out front," he responded, shaking his head.

"I thought maybe you'd have some stashed in the backroom."

Sam eyed me suspiciously. "You working a case, Jim?"

"Yeah, the Mauston death. It seems his wife wants to prove it was murder and not a suicide."

"Is that what you think? That it was a murder?" As far as I could tell, his interest was just curiosity.

"Don't know yet. I've just started poking my nose in things. It does seem a little fishy, though."

"So what's this got to do with Chinatown?"

"Probably nothing, Sam. It's just that Mauston spent time out in the Orient, China, French Indochina, Burma, places like that. It's possible that he rubbed someone out there the wrong way and it caught up with him. I thought you might have heard something."

"All I know about it is what I read in the *Chronicle*."

"You ever do any business with Mauston?"

"Some, not much. Most of what he dealt in was high-end merchandise, real antiques, works of art, that kind of thing, not this junk. He mostly sold it to interior decorators and art dealers out east. Occasionally he'd bring in a shipment for wholesale. I've bought stuff from him off and on, but like I said not much."

"How was he. As a businessman, I mean?"

"He had a good reputation. Always paid his bills on time, treated his employees decently. I know a couple of Chinese girls that work in his office. I've never heard anything bad from them. As far as I know, there's never been any rumors of him being involved in anything illegal like opium or bringing in illegals. He was a businessman; buy low, sell high, just like me, but from what I know, he played it straight. At least since he's been in San Francisco. Certainly, nothing that might lead to murder."

"Yeah, Sam. That's the impression I've been getting. This stuff he imported, though. There wouldn't have been anything that he brought in that maybe he shouldn't have?"

"Like I said, I never heard of him dealing in drugs."

"No, not that, but maybe some of these antiques, maybe the original owners didn't want to part with them. Maybe some stuff with religious significance."

"You mean like some jewel plucked from the head of an idol or something like that?"

"Yeah. Something like that." Even as I said it, I knew it sounded silly.

"You've been reading too many trashy novels, Jim. Too much Sax Rohmer."

"You're the second person to tell me that today."

"Trust me, Jim, there aren't any secret Asian societies out to take over the world. There aren't any Fu Manchu's, not in real life."

"What about the Japs?"

"Most of the Japs I know are only interested in growing melons. The only beef they have that I know of is with the Italians, and that's because they grow melons, too. At least the ones around here. I wouldn't know anything about the ones over there," he said nodding vaguely in a westerly direction towards the Orient. "I've never been farther west than the Golden Gate."

"So you don't think there's anything to the idea that Mauston was killed by a Chinese?"

"Mauston was killed with a gun, wasn't he?"

"Yeah. A .25 caliber automatic."

"There you go. If he'd been killed by a Chinaman, he'd have had his throat slit with a dagger, or been poisoned with some gas. Or maybe he'd have stepped onto a trap door and been dropped into the bay." I could see that Sam was enjoying himself recounting scenes from the movies.

"Okay. I have to admit; it does seem pretty crazy when you put it like that, Sam."

"Like I said, you've been reading the wrong books, Jim. You should read Charlie Chan. It's still crap, but at least the guy with the brains is a Chinaman."

"Okay, Okay. The joke's on me. It's just that I'm trying to find an angle here and not having much luck, Sam. I don't have any suspects, and I don't have much in the way of a motive, either. I've yet to find that Mauston had any enemies, and as things stand, no one really profits from his death. His wife can't even collect the insurance on him unless I can prove that it was murder."

"Sounds like you've got a real mystery on your hands, Jim."

"Yeah. So what would your Charlie Chan say in a case like this?"

Sam looked thoughtful for a moment.

"You know, I'm not sure, but I think if old Charlie were on the case he wouldn't be looking for foreigners, he'd be looking for someone closer to home."

I thought about that. It made some sort of sense.

"Charlie might be on to something there, Sam."

It was getting on towards noon by the time I hit the street again. I realized that I was hungry. More importantly, for once, thanks to Mrs. Mauston, I had enough money in my pocket that I didn't have to scrimp. I beat down the urge to have a liquid lunch and settled on a corner diner not too far from my office.

I was early enough to find a stool at the counter. A waitress, a blonde whose hair color came out of a bottle, deposited a menu in front of me with a smile. I smiled back. She was probably just angling for a tip, but I was in an expansive mood.

I'd been living on a diet of grilled cheese sandwiches lately, but I decided to splurge.

"What can I get for you, honey?" the waitress asked when she came back to take my order.

"I'll have a hamburger with a slice of raw onion, French fries and a cup of coffee to wash it down."

"Care to add a slice of cheese to the burger. It's ten cents extra."

I thought about it for a moment before replying, "Why not? I'm feeling rich."

"I like a man that knows his own mind," she said as she wrote up the order. "It'll be right up."

I watched her as she turned to pass the order ticket through the window to the kitchen. She wasn't bad looking from that angle. But who was I kidding, she was just a waitress trying to get a quarter tip, and I was just a two-bit private dick trying to make sense out of a man's death.

Part of the problem was that the picture I was forming of Mauston was full of contradictions. The papers had painted him as having had some sort of romantic soldier-of-fortune past running around the backcountry of the Orient having wild adventures. But for the last dozen years or so he'd been a successful businessman doing nothing more exciting than making the occasional trip to the Orient to buy up antiques and art for his import business, at least according to Lomax. It was almost like they were two different people. So which one had been the real Charles Mauston? I didn't have an answer to that question yet, and I wasn't convinced that it mattered as far as his murder went.

The more I thought about it, the suicide angle didn't make sense. People don't usually do away with themselves unless they're broke, in bad health, or frustrated in love. From what Lomax had told me, Mauston hadn't had any money problems and had been in reasonably good health. As for love, he'd been married to a good looking woman twenty years his junior. If the marriage hadn't been a happy one, why had he been carrying an insurance policy worth two-hundred and fifty gees?

Had the marriage been a happy one? It didn't take much imagination to see Mrs. Mauston not being satisfied by a husband who was more interested in his business than in socializing. She'd struck me as the kind of woman who'd enjoy a night on the town more than curling up with a good book. Maybe I was wrong about that, but I wouldn't bet on it. Still, that didn't necessarily mean it had been a point of friction between them. Lots of older men are perfectly happy to have their wives wined and dined by someone else as long as they get what they want out of the marriage. Had Mauston been one of them?

The problem was I hadn't known Charles Mauston. All I knew about him was what I had heard second hand from his wife and Lomax. Had there been something going on between Lomax and Mrs. Mauston? In our conversation, he'd referred to her by her first name. Did that mean anything? Or was that only natural, considering she was his partner's wife?

Even if there had been something between Lomax and Mrs. Mauston, it didn't seem likely that Mr. Mauston would commit suicide out of despair. It seemed more likely, that given his past, that it would have been Mrs. Mauston or Lomax, or the both of them, who would have been the ones that ended up dead. But it all came back to the fact that I didn't know how Mr. Mauston would have reacted.

These unproductive musings were interrupted by the waitress dropping my lunch on the counter in front of me.

"Here you are, sugar. Ketchup's next to you. If you need anything else, just holler."

I'd gone from honey to sugar in five minutes. I didn't know if that meant anything or not. "Thanks, I'm fine for right now."

I was struggling to get some of the ketchup out of the bottle and onto my plate when someone took the stool next to me. I looked up and saw that it was Lt. Miller.

It might have been a coincidence. The Hall of Justice wasn't that far from the diner, and it was lunchtime. Even Homicide detectives have to eat.

"How's the burger?"

"I'll let you know in a second," I said as a dollop of ketchup finally landed on the beef patty.

Our witty conversation was interrupted by the waitress.

"What can I get you, honey?" So the waitress called him honey, too. I was suddenly disillusioned.

"Ham and Swiss on rye. Mustard and hold the mayo. And a cup of coffee."

She poured a cup of coffee from the urn on the back counter and set it in front of Miller. She topped off mine at the same time.

Miller dropped a spoonful of sugar and enough cream into his coffee to turn it tan. I would have expected him to drink it black, but maybe it was a Midwestern thing.

"Still working the Mauston case?"

"Seeing as how I just got hired yesterday, yeah, I'm still working the case."

"Find out anything?" Miller said as he filched a French fry.

"Not much. Nobody at his company could think of a reason he'd want to kill himself."

"Still, he ended up dead." Miller grabbed another French fry.

"Look, if you're going to keep swiping my fries, I'm going to have to bill the city."

"Sorry, the wife's been trying to get me to lose weight, so she doesn't feed me enough at home."

My fries were saved by the arrival of Miller's sandwich. He took a couple of big bites, washing it down with coffee.

"So what's your take on this Lomax guy? I assume you talked to him?" Miller asked after he set down his cup.

"I didn't like him. He's too smooth for my taste, but maybe that's just his mustache. I've never trusted guys with mustaches like that."

"Yeah, that was my impression, too," Miller grinned.

"But Lomax has an alibi, doesn't he?"

"Yeah, he was out of town. Salt Lake City."

"You checked up on that, of course?"

"Sure thing. We're not chumps, you know. The Salt Lake City police confirmed that he was staying at a hotel there. He didn't check out until the day after Mauston died. He booked a sleeper on the overnight train from there. We checked up on that, too. I talked to the conductor and the sleeping car attendant. Lomax was on that train."

"Too bad. He would have made a great suspect."

"Yeah, that's what I thought, too, but no such luck."

"So where does that leave us?"

"It leaves us with a dead guy who was alone in his office late at night. He was shot with a pistol he'd bought for his wife."

"Speaking of the wife, where was she at the time?"

"I thought she was your client, not a suspect," Miller commented.

"Just covering all the bases, lieutenant."

"The wife says she was home all that evening. Her maid confirmed that, and there's no reason to doubt either one of them."

"Well, I guess I can rule her out, then."

"Face it, Tolliver, maybe Mauston didn't shoot himself, but if he didn't, neither one of us has got a clue as to who did."

"You're not much help, are you?"

"That's not my job. It's been nice talking to you, Tolliver, but I've got to get back to the hall."

Miller got up, sipped the last of his coffee and left. It was only then that I realized he hadn't paid for his lunch. When the waitress brought the check, I saw that she had added Miller's bill onto mine. I'd have to remember to add it to my expenses on my report for Mrs. Mauston. I dropped enough to cover the bill on the counter and added a couple of quarters for a tip.

6.

I decided to walk back to the office to give my lunch a chance to digest. I find that walking provides me time to think, and I had a lot to think about. I didn't get a lot of thinking done, though. As I walked up Market Street, I had a feeling that I was being followed. I paused a couple of times in front of store windows to take a look behind me, but if I was being tailed, whoever it was knew what they were doing because I couldn't spot them.

I took a detour of a couple of blocks down one of the streets north of Market that angle into it, not so much as an attempt to shake my tail, but more to try to identify them, but I didn't have any luck. The only guy that I kept noticing was short, overweight and in his forties. He was dressed in a brown suit and hat and was carrying a briefcase. He looked like an insurance salesman. Of course, when you think about it, what better disguise could a tail have.

I was warm by the time I got to the building that holds my office, and the relative dark of the lobby came as a relief, even if it wasn't much cooler than it had been outside. I checked with the girl on the switchboard, and there was a message waiting for me. It was from Mrs. Mauston, saying that she wanted me to give her a call.

I rode the elevator up to my office, hung my jacket on the coat rack and picked up the phone.

"This is James Tolliver," I told the maid when she answered the phone. "Mrs. Mauston asked me to call her."

"I'll see if she's in," the maid replied. She had the kind of accent you find in some small Midwestern towns where everybody is Norwegian or Swedish.

A few moments later I heard, "Mr. Tolliver, thank you for calling me back so quickly."

"I just got back to the office. I spent the morning at Far Eastern asking questions. Not that I got much in the way of answers, but I can tell you what I've found so far if you'd like?"

"I'd rather not discuss the matter over the phone, Mr. Tolliver. Would it be possible for you to drop by my place to discuss things? Say around five o'clock?"

"That's fine by me, though I'm not sure that there's that much to discuss yet. I've had less than a day to work on the case."

"I appreciate that, Mr. Tolliver. I'll tell you what. I'll have a cocktail waiting for you to make it worth your while."

"The client's always right, Mrs. Mauston. I'll be there at five."

"I'll be expecting you, Mr. Tolliver. Good-bye."

The line went dead before I could say goodbye in return, but Mrs. Mauston hadn't sounded a bit like a grieving widow.

I had to make a report to my client, and I still had the feeling that I didn't know enough about Charles Mauston to know which direction the investigation was heading. Nothing in his current life seemed to provide a reason for his murder. That pretty much only left the past, the time that he'd spent in the Orient, particularly in Shanghai at the end of the war. That was a time of crisis, of disruption, of upheaval. If there were any period in his life where he might have made an enemy, that would be it.

The problem was that neither his wife nor his partner had known him back then. They'd only been able to give me the sketchiest overview of that portion of his life. The Chinese angle had proved to be a dead end, but that still left the Russians. I needed to talk to someone who'd actually been there at that time. Fortunately, I knew someone who fit the bill, and he only worked a few blocks away.

Alexei Andreavich owned a little antique shop on Geary. It wasn't much of a place, but Alexei seemed to get by. The word on the street was that he didn't ask too many questions about what he bought or sold. To my knowledge, nothing had ever been proved against him, but I didn't doubt that the provenance of at least some of his stock was dubious.

I'd first run into Alexei when I was trying to track down a stolen statue for a client. Alexei hadn't had the statue, but he had had some ideas as to who did. They didn't do me any good, though, the statue was gone by the time I got there.

From our conversations, I knew that Alexei had been in Shanghai at the end of the war. He'd been able to get out because his mother had been English and he'd been able to obtain a British passport. There was a chance that he might know something about Mauston that the papers or Lomax didn't. It was at least worth a shot, and his shop wasn't far from my office.

Unlike the showroom of Far Eastern Specialties, Alexei's shop was filled to the point that there was barely room to walk down the narrow aisle that ran down the center of it. Chairs were stacked on top of each other, or on top of tables. The walls were covered with paintings, mostly not very good, and shelves and a couple of display cases full of old bric-a-brac stretched the length of one of the sides.

Alexei appeared from a small room at the back when he heard me enter. He was a smallish man, with just enough hair to comb over the balding spot on the top of his head. He wore a pair of pince-nez glasses with a black ribbon that went around his neck. As a concession to the season, he wore a suit of faded white flannel.

"Why if it isn't Jim Tolliver! On the trail of another statue?" He had an undefinable accent, part British, part French, part something else that may have been of his own invention. I knew for a fact that he spoke fluent French and Russian, and enough German and Spanish to get by.

"No, I'm in the market for some information."

"Information. Now that *is* a precious commodity. How can I help you out?"

"You were in Shanghai after the war, weren't you?"

"I had that misfortune. Along with half the nobility of Russia. At least those that survived. What about it? Certainly, you don't want to drag up memories of the bad old days."

"When you were there did you ever run across a man by the name of Charles Mauston?"

"Charles Mauston? Not by any chance the one that committed suicide?"

"Yes, that's the one. Except, I'm not so sure that it was suicide."

"How intriguing. You must tell me more, Jimmy."

"Well, that's just it. I don't know much, other than the fact that he didn't seem to have any reason to kill himself. That's why I'm trying to find out something about his past."

"I see. Well, I knew Mauston back then, or at least I knew *of* him. Except that he wasn't going by the name Charles. I think he mostly used Thomas or Tommy."

Mauston's middle name had been Thomas. "Interesting. What can you tell me about him?"

"Not a lot, I'm afraid. As I said, I didn't really know him. But everyone more or less knew *of* him."

"Oh?"

"Well, he was a colorful figure back in those days. Always traveling from one place to another. Shanghai, Saigon, Singapore, Djakarta, Rangoon. He was what you Americans call a real wheeler-dealer. Always arranging to buy something in one place and sell it at another for a substantial profit. You have to remember that the Orient was a wide open place in those days, not like it is today. Especially in China. No real government. You could get away with anything if you knew the right people, and Mauston seemed to know all the right people. He'd been doing it since just after the turn of the century from what I understand. Knew all sorts of shady characters and who to bribe and how much."

"That doesn't sound much like the man who was killed. From what I've seen he lived pretty quietly here in San Francisco. What would make a man change like that?"

"Old age, Jimmy. I think he saw that things were ripe for a change, and not for the better. He'd made his pile of money, particularly right after the war. From what I hear he wanted to live to enjoy it."

"So he was afraid for his life?"

"No, not in the sense that he thought someone was going to kill him, but in that sort of environment—Well things can happen, particularly when you've got money, and other people haven't. I think it was more a case of leaving before the law of averages caught up with him."

"But he did make any enemies out there?"

"Oh, I'm sure he did. One couldn't very well be in the kind of business he was and not rub some people the wrong way. But I don't remember ever hearing about anything particular. For all his playing fast and loose, as far as I know, he was actually pretty honest in his dealings. A lot of the natives, the people in the backwaters, swore by him because he didn't try to cheat them."

"I know that the papers mentioned something about rumors that he'd made a lot of money out of the Russians trying to flee the Bolsheviks. Anything to that?"

"Oh, that part's true enough. You have to understand the situation. Shanghai was the end of the line for those trying to stay one step ahead of Lenin and his lot. They could get there easily enough, but once there, getting out was a lot harder. Half of them had lost their papers, and the Russian embassy certainly wasn't going to be of any help in that department. To get exit visas out of the Chinese, you had to know who to pay off. Well, Mauston knew who to deal with, who to pay off, and what ships he could put people on when they didn't have the right papers. In his way, he was quite a humanitarian. There are a lot of people who'd still be stuck in Shanghai or dead if he hadn't helped them get away to Suez or Cape Town, or wherever. I think that his experiences in that period have a lot to do with why he left the Orient. It changed him. Of course, it changed a lot of people."

"But of course he took his cut—"

Alexei looked at me as if I was a simpleton. "Of course he did. He was a businessman, after all, and he had expenses, bribes, payouts, forgers. But unlike some, he usually delivered."

"So you don't know of anyone that might hold a grudge?"

"No. Though I'm sure that there were some that ended up disappointed. Not every plan goes as intended. There were probably some who were betrayed by people down the chain or held up for more money along the way. But I'm not personally aware of anyone that that happened to. I'm afraid you'll have to ask elsewhere for that information."

"Any ideas on where?"

"I'm not sure you're going to have much luck in that direction, Jimmy. The émigré community is pretty well dispersed in America these days, at least the ones that came through Shanghai. And there's a lot of distrust. For one thing, no one is sure who might be a Soviet agent, or who might collaborate to protect family that got left behind. What groups there are tend to be pretty closed-mouthed if you get what I mean."

"But you must know someone I could talk to—"

"Well, there is a place here in San Francisco. It's a sort of Russian tea room where some of the older émigrés congregate. You could try there. But I wouldn't hold my breath."

"Where is this place?"

"It's called the White Russian. It was started by a colonel that was in the Imperial cavalry. It's run by his three sons now. Here, I'll write the address down for you."

He scribbled something on the back of a business card and handed it to me.

"Thanks, Alexei. I'll remember this." I pocketed the card and dropped a twenty on the counter.

"Frankly, Jimmy. I'd just as soon you'd forget this conversation ever took place. And whatever you do, please don't mention my name in conjunction with this business."

"It's like that, is it?"

"Yes, it's like that. People might get the wrong idea. These people have lived all their lives in fear of the secret police, first the czar's, then Bolsheviks'. Not knowing who to trust is part of their upbringing."

"This is America, Alexei."

"But some of these people are still living mentally in the old country. Just keep me out of it. And watch yourself, Jimmy. Watch yourself."

I walked down to Market and caught a taxi. As I was riding in the cab, I thought about what I'd learned from Alexei, which wasn't much. Did the whole Russian angle even make sense? Shanghai had been nearly twenty years earlier. If someone had been in the market for vengeance, why had they waited this long? I had a feeling I was on a wild goose chase, but that's the way it is sometimes on an investigation. You never know which leads are going to turn into something until you follow them through to the end.

I didn't have much time to think about it before the cab stopped to let me out. I paid off the driver and headed for The White Russian.

7.

The address Alexei had given me was for a Queen Anne house on Telegraph Hill, a few blocks north of Broadway. The house had been painted recently, as had the white picket fence around the small front yard. A carefully tended flower bed formed a border in front of the two-story building. It didn't particularly look to me like a den of international intrigue.

There was no sign out front, but when I had passed through the gate in the fence and walked up to the porch, there was one next to the front door. It said something in Cyrillic lettering which I couldn't read. Below that, in English, it proclaimed "The White Russian" in smaller letters.

An overhead bell tinkled gaily when I went through the door. I found myself in a small hallway. There was a stairway leading up, but it was blocked off with a red velvet rope. An archway to the left led into what was obviously the tea room proper.

This was a cheerful room, brightly lit with large, south facing windows. Arranged about the place were a number of mismatched tables and chairs. The walls, what I could see of them, had been painted a pale yellow and were covered by framed photos of a Russia that had ceased to exist with the revolution. On the back wall, there was a portrait of Czar Nickolas flanked by an Imperial Russian flag and crossed cavalry sabers. Underneath the czar was a sideboard on which stood a gleaming silver samovar.

The only customers were an older couple sitting in the bay window. The man was reading a French newspaper of uncertain vintage while the woman was engaged in some embroidery.

As I entered a giant of a man appeared from somewhere in the rear of the house. He was wearing grey riding breeches and a tunic of the same color which had empty cartridge loops over the left breast. His head was shaved, and I could see the outline of a faded bullet scar just over his left ear. He approached me, said something in Russian that I couldn't understand and pointed at one of the tables. I took that as an invitation and sat.

A moment later he returned, this time with a small towel draped over his arm. Again he asked something in Russian. I shrugged and said "tea." He repeated the question, or at least I thought he did, then switched to French. His French was better than mine. He was asking for my order. My French was a bit rusty, but I managed to get across the idea that I wanted a cup of tea.

The Cossack waiter retreated to the sideboard where he poured a cup of tea from the samovar and then laid it on the table next to me. He withdrew, but returned a moment later and added a small plate with two tiny triangles of toast with a thin smear of a black substance that I presumed was caviar. Having deposited that, he went over to the couple in the window and made an inquiry in Russian. The man replied in the same language with a shake of his head. The Cossack bowed and withdrew to the rear of the house.

The tea was strong and bitter. I was about to try the toast when another man appeared from the rear. He was younger than the Cossack and shorter by several inches. His head wasn't shaved, and his hair was slicked back, but his features shared the same Slavic affinity as the waiter. His suit, though showing signs of wear, was well tailored and of good material.

Without a word he pulled out the other chair at my table and sat, his legs crossed. From his jacket pocket, he extracted a silver cigarette case, opened it and withdrew a French cigarette. This he placed in his mouth and then lit from a wooden match that he struck on the table leg. He took a puff on the cigarette, holding it in that reversed way of which foreign movie villains are so fond. While he did this, the Cossack came out from the back, poured a cup of tea, and set it on the table in front of him. After that, he took up a position of attention at the archway leading to the front hall. A moment later, another Cossack that could have been a twin of the first appeared to stand at the door leading into the back.

As he smoked, he examined me with much the same expression that one would use with a piece of garbage on the street. Finally he said:

"You are with the police?"

His English was clear but accented, the word "police" being pronounced with a longer "e" than an American would use.

I looked back at him. I'm not sure what expression I used, but it wasn't one of approval. "No, I am not with the police."

"Ah," he responded. "Then you are with the secret police."

"We don't have secret police in this country."

"You Americans. So naïve. Of course, you have the secret police. Every country has the secret police. Only in some places, they are more secret than others."

"Let's cut to the chase, Ivan. I'm not with the police, secret or otherwise. My name is James Tolliver, and I'm a private investigator licensed by the State of California." I reached inside my jacket a pulled out my license to prove it.

Ivan took my license and examined it closely, though what he expected to find, I don't know. After a minute or so he handed it back.

"So, Mr. James Tolliver, you are, as they say, a private eye. Which is nothing more than a policeman for hire. By the way, my name is not Ivan. That is my brother, the one by the entry. My other brother's name is Boris. My name is Mikhail."

"My apologies, Mikhail."

"Now what is it you want, Mr. James Tolliver? I know that you Americans are not fond of tea."

"It's not bad, actually, but you're right, I'm more of a coffee man, myself, when I'm not drinking something stronger. I'm looking for some information. An acquaintance of mine suggested this might be the place for it."

"Your acquaintance was mistaken. We sell only tea here. Tea and small sandwiches and cakes. By the way, who is this acquaintance? Perhaps I know him and can correct his notion as to what we deal in at the White Russian."

"Oh, I don't think that will be necessary. But getting back to the reason I'm here, I'm looking into the death of Charles Mauston."

"The one who killed himself?" Mikhail said cautiously.

"That's what the police think. Me, I'm not so sure."

"And what does the death of this man have to do with The White Russian, Mr. Tolliver?"

"Probably nothing. It's just that Mauston was out in Shanghai after the war. It's my understanding that he had dealings with some of your people. Helping get them out of China, arranging transportation, papers, that kind of thing."

"And making a handsome profit at the same time."

"Probably. He was, after all, a businessman."

"And what does this have to do with me?"

"I'm just trying to get in touch with anyone that might have known Mauston in China, or that might have had dealings with him."

"Why, Mr. Tolliver? What do you hope to discover?"

"Someone killed Mauston. They shot him in his office late at night. Nothing was stolen, so robbery wasn't a motive. It must have been something else. And whoever it was, Mauston must have known them, or he wouldn't have let them up into his office. I'm investigating the possibility that whoever killed him might have known him in Shanghai."

"So, you come here thinking to find his killer?"

"This *is* the center of the Russian émigré community in San Francisco. I've got to start somewhere."

"Take a look around you, Mr. Tolliver," Mikhail said with a wide sweep of his hand. "Do the old couple in the window look like assassins? Do you think maybe the old lady has a pistol hidden in her sewing basket? Do you have any idea who they are?"

Mikhail's voice had risen. The old couple looked nervously in our direction.

"No, I don't," I said softly. "Maybe you'd care to tell me."

"Before the Bolsheviks, he was the directory of the Trans Siberian railroad. A big man, a friend of princes. Now he spends his days sitting there pretending to read old newspapers friends give him when they are done with them. They have one cup of tea each because that's all they can afford. They sit here all day because they have nowhere else to go except a tiny rented room. Do you really think such people are killers?"

"I didn't mean to imply—"

"No, I'm sure you didn't, Mr. Tolliver. I assure you that Georgy Feodorovich didn't kill your Mr. Mauston. I'm pretty sure his wife didn't either. You ask about Shanghai, Mr. Tolliver. I'll tell you about Shanghai. Of course, I was just a child at the time, but I remember riding in a train across Siberia. Everyone on the train was trying to get out and afraid that at any junction the Red cavalry would stop it and take everyone out and shoot them. They were the cream of Russian society, nobles and generals, professional men, businessmen, and they'd left everything they'd worked all their lives for, and all they had left was what they could pack in a suitcase. And then they got to Shanghai, and they thought their problems were over. But they weren't. I remember my parents talking about it. You couldn't leave Shanghai without the proper papers, and you couldn't get the proper papers because the government that was supposed to issue them didn't exist anymore, and the Bolshevik government that replaced it certainly wasn't going to help a bunch of capitalists and imperialists. So we sat and waited, and waited, spending our dwindling resources until we could make a deal with men like this Charles Mauston to get fake papers and passage on any tramp steamer going someplace else. Such things could be arranged, of course, if you had enough money. But no one had enough money, so they gave up their jewels and family heirlooms and anything else that could be converted into ready cash. And yes, some of them did manage to get out of Shanghai, but some of them are still there, waiting for who knows what. Maybe the Japanese. So ask me if I care whether this Mauston killed himself or if someone else did the job for him."

"Look, Mikhail, I'm just doing a job. Life isn't fair. I know it and you know it. I lost friends of mine in the woods of the Ardennes."

"So you were in the war like my brothers fighting the Germans. At least you didn't have your own people stabbing you in the back like they did. Let me suggest something to you, Mr. Private Eye; if this Mauston was killed you shouldn't be looking amongst the poor refuse of Mother Russia for the killer. If anything, you should be looking amongst the agents of the Soviets. Mauston helped a lot of good people get out of Shanghai, people the Bolsheviks wanted to put in prison or execute. Maybe the Soviets killed him. They've killed for less."

"This is America, Mikhail."

"And you don't have foreign spies in America?"

"You asked your questions. I gave you answers. If you don't like them—"

Mikhail looked at me, then stubbed out his cigarette on the saucer of his teacup.

"I'm sorry, Mr. Tolliver. Perhaps I got overly excited. I try not to think about the old days, about what might have been. That was almost two decades ago. We were some of the lucky ones, my brothers and I, and our parents. We got out. My parents had enough money left to set up this little tea shop, but never any more. They're gone now, my parents. The old people, the ones that are still living, come and drink their tea and talk about the old times, the better times, but that's all they do. And the rest of us, the younger ones, we just try to get by. We don't have time for vendettas or revenge. Even if we did, it wouldn't be against some Shanghai middleman. It would be against the Bolsheviks. To answer your question, Mr. Tolliver, I don't know of anyone that had anything against this Mauston. But even if I did, I probably wouldn't tell you about them. It's none of my business. My business is tea."

Mikhail looked as if he'd exhausted himself talking. It was pretty clear I wasn't going to get anything more from him. I certainly wasn't going to get anything from his brothers.

"Speaking of tea, how much do I owe you? Your brother wasn't exactly clear on that point."

"You owe me nothing, Mr. Tolliver. It's on the house. Just one thing, though."

"What's that?"

"The next time you get a craving for tea I suggest you go somewhere else. Do we understand each other?"

"I think we do."

I got up and left Mikhail sitting there lighting another cigarette. The Cossack, Boris or Ivan, I couldn't remember which, escorted me to the door, shutting it firmly behind me.

I checked my watch. It wasn't quite four o'clock, just enough time to get back to my apartment, take a quick shower, and change my shirt. I'd spent the day pounding the pavement, and I wanted to look my best for Mrs. Mauston.

8.

I took a taxi to the address Mrs. Mauston had given me. I had been expecting it to be one of the older Victorian or Queen Anne houses so common in San Francisco, but when I paid off the cabbie, I found myself in front of a rather posh looking Art Deco apartment building that must have been put up just before the stock market crash.

The doorman, and yes, there was a doorman, gave me the fisheye as if suggesting I go around to the tradesman's entrance in the rear, but when I said Mrs. Mauston was expecting me he picked up a phone in the entryway. A short conversation ensued which I couldn't overhear, but the results must have been satisfactory because after he hung up, he opened the inner door and bowed me through.

"Third floor, Mr. Tolliver, Apartment 3A. The elevator is straight ahead."

The elevator was self-service. I pushed the button for the third floor. The door closed and carried me smoothly upward. When the door opened again, I found myself facing a carpeted hallway. Whoever the interior designer was, they had had an odd color sense because the carpet had an abstract floral pattern that was mostly mauve while the walls were plastered in sort of faded green with a rose band about eye-level. Aerodynamic looking sconces in brushed nickel provided illumination every dozen feet or so. It was all very clean and modern looking.

Apartment 3A turned out to be in the right front corner facing the street. A neatly typed card was on the door. It hadn't been changed yet because it announced that this was the residence of Mr. Chas. Mauston. There was a doorbell next to the door. I pressed it. A few moments later the door was opened by the maid, a tallish woman with broad shoulders and graying blonde hair who looked to be in her mid-forties.

"May I take your hat, Mr. Tolliver?" she asked after closing the door behind me. Evidently, it was the same woman who had answered the phone when I called as her accent was vaguely

Scandinavian as if she'd been in this country a long time or came from someplace like Minnesota where everyone talked like that. I handed her my hat, which she placed on a tall, angular table next to the door.

"This way, please." She sounded rigid and efficient in the way that only northern Europeans can manage.

I followed her wake to a large sitting room that must have taken up the entire front of the apartment. Glass doors along one wall gave out onto a small balcony. You could just catch a glimpse of the bay over the top of the building across the street.

Considering Mr. Mauston's occupation, I would have expected the furnishings to have been Oriental. Instead, they were streamlined, modern, and obviously expensive. It struck me as tasteful but a bit sterile. I suspected that Mrs. Mauston had been responsible for the décor.

Mrs. Mauston had been sitting in a chair with her back to the balcony, but she rose as I entered. She was wearing something clingy in a light green fabric that covered but didn't conceal her figure. The color went well with her hair, which was probably why she had chosen it.

"That will be all, Ada." The way she said it was more of a statement than an order.

"Yes, ma'am," the maid replied and left the room.

"Thank you for coming on such short notice, Mr. Tolliver. May I offer you a cocktail?"

"I wouldn't refuse."

While Mrs. Mauston busied herself mixing the drinks, I took the opportunity to look around. It was all very tasteful and harmonious, but somehow lacking in personality. Everything was neat and obviously in its place, but there were none of the little personal touches one typically finds, no family pictures, no knick-knacks, no souvenirs. In particular, there was nothing recognizable as having belonged to the late Mr. Mauston. Was that why he had spent so many late nights at his office?

She turned back to me and handed me a glass with ice floating in a brown liquid. A very red cherry was jostled by the ice cubes. "I hope you like it." She must have caught me looking around because there was the hint of a smile on her austere face.

I took a sip of the drink to cover my embarrassment at having been caught out inspecting the place. It was cool and smooth, the booze in it top shelf.

"Why don't you tell me what you've found so far, Mr. Tolliver?"

"Not much, at this point, but then, I've only been on the case for a day. I've read the newspaper accounts and talked to the detective who handled the case—"

"Lt. Miller, I believe."

"Yes. Lt. Miller. I know him, somewhat. He's good at his job. Not like some of the bums at the Hall of Justice. There was nothing in the papers or police report to indicate foul-play of any sort, but then you probably already knew all that, didn't you, Mrs. Mauston."

"Yes. Lt. Miller kept me informed as to what the police had found, which was that there was nothing to indicate that my husband hadn't killed himself. But that was why I hired you, Mr. Tolliver."

"Just out of curiosity, Mrs. Mauston, why did you hire me? Mine's not the first name listed in the Yellow Pages. I mean, you could have easily gone with one of the big national agencies like Continental. They have resources that I can't match."

"Oh, don't sell yourself short, Mr. Tolliver. You've got something of a reputation around town. I asked around a bit, people that I know. Your name came up—"

I wasn't exactly buying into what she was saying. I've had a bit of luck on a few cases, but not the kind that had gotten my name in the papers. And I doubted that many of my former clients traveled in the same circles as Mrs. Mauston. I had the feeling that behind those green eyes, eyes that were pale green like her dress, that she was playing some game of her own with me, a game where she was the one making the rules. I wasn't sure what the game was, but for five hundred bucks I could afford to play games.

"Getting back to my report, Mrs. Mauston, I interviewed Nilgren, the office manager, and your husband's partner, Lomax. Neither of them could suggest any reason why your husband should do away with himself."

She seemed to react to that, or at least that's what she wanted me to believe.

"I'm sorry if I've upset you, Mrs. Mauston."

"No, that's quite alright, Mr. Tolliver. I understand that you have to look at these matters analytically." She looked away into a corner of the room.

"As far as I've been able to determine, your husband's affairs were all in order; his health was not a problem, the business was making money. In short, there doesn't seem to be any reason for him to want to kill himself. Which, of course, is what you want me to prove, isn't it?"

"Yes. Exactly."

"Out of curiosity, just how well do you know Mr. Lomax?"

"You seem to be a very curious sort of person, Mr. Tolliver." Again, there was just a hint of a smile. She seemed well aware of the double meaning of that statement, had intended it.

"It sort of comes with the territory, Mrs. Mauston. Curiosity is what makes a detective, at least a good one. Of course, it can get you into trouble sometimes."

"I'm sure it has," she replied impishly.

"You haven't answered my question, though."

"No, I haven't, have I." She paused as if trying to decide how much of herself to reveal. It wasn't much. "Of course, I know him through Charles, but I can't say that we socialized all that much. The occasional dinner with the three of us, that sort of thing. Once or twice, Edward has taken me to the theatre when Charles didn't feel like it. But, no, I don't know Mr. Lomax all that well. Not on a personal level. Why do you ask?"

"Oh, just curiosity. You do know, that with your husband's death, his share of the business reverts to Lomax? That you won't get anything from the business?"

"Yes. I was aware of that clause in their arrangement." I thought she didn't sound particularly pleased about the fact.

"How well are you set up for money, Mrs. Mauston, ignoring the insurance policy?"

"Oh, I'm not penniless, Mr. Tolliver, if that's what you want to know. Charles had money in the bank, some stocks, whatever they're worth these days, some real estate he held privately outside the business. I won't starve if that's what you're asking. But I won't deny that the insurance money would help me maintain my lifestyle." She waved her hand around the room to emphasize the last point.

"You can see that I've been living quite comfortably, Mr. Tolliver. My husband was careful with his money, but he wasn't tight-fisted. I've always had enough for clothes and entertainment. Which are reasons for me *not* to wish my husband dead, if you are considering me as a suspect."

I took another sip of the cocktail. "Oh, I haven't gotten to the suspect stage yet. I haven't even convinced myself that there's been a crime, Mrs. Mauston."

"I'm sorry, Mr. Tolliver. This whole business has me on edge. Not knowing about the future—the insurance policy—"

"Were you aware that the insurance company wouldn't pay out in a case of suicide, Mrs. Mauston?"

She looked at me, again as if thinking what answer she wanted me to hear.

"Vaguely. I never read the fine print, if that's what you want to know. But I believe most policies have clauses to that effect. Isn't that true?"

"I think it's a pretty common practice, Mrs. Mauston."

"So I had every reason to keep my husband alive and happy."

"So it would seem."

"You really *do* just say whatever's on your mind, don't you, Mr. Tolliver?"

"I've been known to do that."

"Doesn't that get you into trouble?" The hint of a smile was back.

"Frequently."

"I *do* want us to be friends, Mr. Tolliver. I have this feeling that I'm going to need friends." She was jumping back and forth between being the grieving widow and the coquettish kitten so fast that I was getting whiplash.

"I'll do my best."

"I'm sure you will."

"One of the reasons the police thought it might be suicide is the note they found, or rather the start of a note that read 'I intend to put an end to this—' If it wasn't a suicide note, do you have any idea what it might have referred to? What it was that he intended to 'put an end to?' There's a chance that it might be related to his death."

"No. No, I have no idea what Charles meant. Perhaps some business arrangement—" Her voice had become cold, dismissive. I had the feeling that I wasn't going to get any more out of her about the note. I changed the subject.

"Is there anything more that you can tell me about Mr. Mauston's past? Anything that might provide a motive for someone to want him dead?"

"No. But then I didn't know much about Charles' past. I only met him shortly before we were married, and by then he had settled down here in San Francisco. He never talked much about his days out in the Orient except for an occasional amusing anecdote. But he never seemed concerned about it, either. I suppose he might have made an enemy or two out there at some point, but if he did, he never mentioned the fact to me."

"The papers mentioned rumors that he had made quite a bit of money dealing with Russian refugees in Shanghai after the war. Was that true?"

"You can't believe all you read in the papers, Mr. Tolliver, but I think there is some truth to those rumors. After all, there were a lot of Russian aristocrats who escaped the Bolsheviks with just the clothes on their backs and whatever jewelry and valuables they could stuff in their pockets. Charles would have known how to convert those valuables into ready money and obtain the proper papers, and passage out of China. He'd been doing it for years. But from what I understand, most of those people would have been glad of any assistance he might have offered."

"Even if he made a big profit off of them?"

"That's what businessmen do, isn't it Mr. Tolliver?"

"So you don't think that there was some Russian count gunning for your husband?"

"You almost make it sound romantic, Mr. Tolliver, but no, not to my knowledge. Charles was just a businessman." There was just a hint of disdain and disappointment in her voice. "You don't really think that Charles might have been killed by some foreigner, do you?"

I found her responses curious. During our initial interview, she had alluded to his death having something to do with his time in China. Given her position, I would have thought that even the hint of something like that would have been music to her ears. Instead, it was almost as if she was trying to steer me away from that line of investigation.

"No, I don't. I looked into it, of course. I had to, but the contacts that I have make it seem extremely unlikely. It's much more likely to be domestic rather than foreign."

"Oh?"

"At least that's what Charlie would advise."

"Charlie?" she said, puzzled.

"Yeah. Charlie, Charlie Chan. A friend of mine in Chinatown told me that Chan would advise me to look closer to home."

"You say the most extraordinary things, Mr. Tolliver."

"I do, don't I," After a pause, I continued, "Is there anything else you can tell me, anything that might explain why your husband was murdered?"

"No. I'm afraid not. If I did know something useful, obviously I'd tell you. Though there is one little thing—"

"Anything might help, Mrs. Mauston. I'm kind of running out of things to investigate."

"Well, it's just this—Mr. Lomax was out of town the night Charles was killed, wasn't he? The police have established that beyond question?"

"Yes. He was in Salt Lake City. The police have checked with the hotel that he was staying at and proved that he arrived in San Francisco on an overnight train from there two days after your husband was killed. Why do you ask?"

"Well, it's probably nothing. It can't mean anything if Edward was in Salt Lake City. It's just that a friend of mine thought she saw Mr. Lomax outside a restaurant here in San Francisco the night Charles died. But if he was in Salt Lake City, she must have been mistaken."

"Probably. She didn't happen to mention which restaurant, did she?"

"The one in the Hotel Alexandria. Does that mean anything?"

"Probably not, but it's something for me to check."

"Surely you don't think that Edward could have had something to do with my husband's death?"

"I don't think anything at this point. As you said, Lomax has an alibi for that night."

The conversation lapsed at the point. I was out of questions, and I sensed that Mrs. Mauston was out of answers.

"I see I've been neglecting my duties as a hostess. Can I mix you another drink, Mr. Tolliver?"

"No, I think I'll take a rain check on that. I should get going."

"That's too bad. We'll have to do this again, Mr. Tolliver. When you have something more to report."

I was going to show myself out, but the maid was at the door to hand me my hat.

Outside, I had the doorman call me a taxi. As I waited, I could have sworn that I saw that same insurance salesman from earlier standing in a doorway across the street. I was about to cross over to confront him when the cab showed up.

9.

I told the cab driver to take me to the *Chronicle* building. I had the picture of Lomax that I had snipped from the paper, but I thought I might need one of higher quality if I was going to try to trace his movements the night Mauston had been killed.

I had the cabbie drop me at the entrance used by employees and paid him off. There was a bored looking watchman sitting behind a desk reading a racing form, but I got past him by looking like I knew where I was going. I nodded when he glanced up for a moment, but he just returned to his paper without acknowledgment.

The photographers at the *Chronicle* usually hung out in a small room in the basement polishing their lenses or playing poker while waiting for an assignment from one of the editors. I knew a couple of them from previous cases, and I was hoping that one of them that owed me a favor would be in. I was in luck.

"Well, if it isn't Jim Tolliver, San Francisco's most private eye. What brings you to the bowels of the earth, Jimmy?"

The guy doing the asking was Floyd Packard, a tall, skinny guy in his early thirties. He was the paper's crime photographer, though that didn't keep him from covering other stories as needed. The other photographers in the room were Sam Flegel who mostly covered City Hall and government and George Bender who took photos for the sports pages. Sam and George were playing a game of gin rummy. I knew them both by sight, and they said hello before returning their attention to their game.

"I just thought I'd see how the other half lived."

"What other half is that?"

"The half that sits on its rear all day and doesn't have to work."

"This from a man who makes his living bent over peeping through keyholes," Floyd said as an aside to the rummy players. "Seriously, Jim. What do you need? You didn't make your way down to our cave just to crack wise."

"I've got a favor to ask."

"See. I thought so," he said, talking to the card players who had looked up suddenly taking an interest. "What is it? Don't tell me you need some photos shot at your wedding."

"No. It's nothing much, really. I'd just like prints of a couple of photographs that appeared in the paper a few weeks back."

"The service desk upstairs can arrange that, Jimmy," Floyd replied.

"The thing is, I'm kind of in a hurry. I'd like to get my hands on the prints tonight. It's in connection with a case I'm working on."

"It'll cost you, Jimmy. Service, while you wait, is extra."

"That's fine by me." I pulled a sawbuck out of my wallet and laid it on Packard's desk. "Will this cover it?"

"I'll need to slip Henry, the boy who works the dark room, a couple of bucks—"

I peeled a couple of singles off and laid them on top of the tenspot.

"This case you're on must be paying pretty good, Jimmy."

"I getting expenses. You're an expense."

"I'm flattered, I think," Floyd responded. "What do you need?"

"I need a picture of Charles Mauston, and one of his partner, Edgar Lomax. The ones that were printed in the paper will do just fine."

"Mauston, the guy that committed suicide?"

"Yeah."

Floyd picked up the phone on his desk. "Henry, get in here. I've got a rush job for you."

A couple of minutes later a kid popped his head in the door. He might have been nineteen. He was wearing a rubberized apron and had a magnifying loupe dangling from a cord around his neck. The expression on his face was halfway between excitement and exasperation.

"What is it, Mr. Packard? I'm kind of busy right now."

"Henry, this is James Tolliver, the famous private investigator. Jim, this is Henry, our current wizard of the darkroom."

I held out my hand. Henry wiped his hand off on his pants and shook.

"Mr. Tolliver is working an important case, and he needs our help. You know those photos that we ran of Charles Mauston and his partner Lomax for that suicide case. He needs prints of those right away. Will five by sevens do, Jim?"

"Sure, that'll be fine. While you're at it, why don't you do a print of Mrs. Mauston, too?"

"But the city desk editor has me doing some prints for the next edition."

"Certainly a bright boy like you can fit in three lousy prints, can't you, Henry?" Packard jibed.

"I guess. If I won't get in trouble."

"There might be a few bucks for you in it."

"Okay. But it will take an hour to let them dry."

"That'll be fine, Henry. You better get to it then, if you've got other work to do as well."

"Yes sir, Mr. Packard," the kid said before he disappeared.

"The kid still thinks I'm important," Packard commented.

"He'll learn better," I responded.

"Say, Tolliver, as long as you've got to hang around for awhile, why don't we play some poker?" Flegel suggested. "Bender here is beating the pants off me at rummy, and I've got to make it back, or the missus will be sore."

"Sure, why not? As long as the stakes aren't too rich."

"We're strictly penny-ante down here," Flegel assured me. "No fancy games, either, just draw."

"Suits me."

We cleared some prints off from the table in the middle of the room, and Flegel produced a fresh deck of cards and a big jar of coins "in case you need to make change." I didn't have much change on me, so I bought a bucks worth.

"Cut for the deal," he said after we'd all gotten seated. Bender cut the low card, so he dealt first.

"So what's the interest, Jim?" Packard asked as he examined his hand. "I thought the cops had decided it was a suicide."

"Yeah, well the cops decide a lot of things that ain't necessarily so. There are a few things about Mauston's death that just don't add up."

"How many cards?" Bender asked.

"I'll take one," Packard said. "Like what?"

I looked at my hand which wasn't much, just a possible inside straight with a two wide hole in the middle.

"I'll take three. Like mostly why he would want to kill himself. He didn't seem to have any money problems or health issues. From what I've heard, Mauston was a pretty tough old bird, not the kind that would elect to take the easy way out. If putting a bullet through your brain is the easy way."

The cards when I got them didn't help, so I folded.

"I'll raise a penny. From what I heard, he had a good-looking wife, too. Is that your angle, Jimmy?"

"My relationship with Mrs. Mauston is purely professional, Floyd. She's retained me to prove that her husband was murdered."

"So it's like that, eh? Murder," Packard said excitedly. Bender had folded along with me, but Flegel anteed up. "I call." Packard had a pair of eights and a king. Flegel had three twos. He pulled in the pot, all ten cents, and started to deal the next hand.

"Who are the suspects, Jimmy? Usually, when a rich guy like that is murdered, it's the wife behind it. But I guess if she's hired you to prove her husband didn't kill himself we can rule her out."

"I haven't got any suspects yet," I responded. "I was just hired yesterday."

"I bet it was the Bolsheviks," Flegel chimed in. "They're behind everything these days. Them or the bankers."

"Nah," Bender retorted. "Bankers don't go around killing people. They just kick them out of hearth and home. I read that this Mauston guy did business with the Orient. He probably crossed one of them Chinese tong gangs."

"You've got it all wrong, George. If a Chinese had killed him, it would have been with a knife. They don't use guns."

"They invented gunpowder, didn't they?" Bender countered.

"Yeah, and all they use it for is firecrackers," Flegel answered.

My next hand was only marginally better than the last, a pair of fives and the jack of diamonds.

"I'll take two. Is this what you put up with all day?" I asked Floyd.

"Pretty much. The only time I get any peace is when I'm out taking pictures."

I lost that hand, too. We spent the next fifteen minutes hashing over the case. Mostly it was the three of them coming up with one wild theory or another and me shooting it down. I didn't really mind. The three guys in that room probably knew as much about what was going on in the city as anyone. After a while, the topic switched to baseball and Stanford's chances in the upcoming football season.

The cards weren't particularly in anyone's favor, and after an hour I was up fifteen cents, Floyd had made four bits while George had lost the most trying to fill an inside straight. The game broke up when Henry returned with the prints.

"Here, let me take a look at them, Henry," Floyd said. He held them up to the light giving them a professional appraisal.

"Good work, kid. Here's your two bucks. And it might be better if you don't mention this to anyone, understand," he said with a wink.

"Sure thing, Mr. Packard."

"Thanks, Henry," I added. "I owe you one."

Packard handed me the stack of prints. They were still slightly damp and smelled of developer. The one of Lomax on top.

"That's your killer, Jim," Floyd pronounced, tapping it with his finger.

"How do you figure?"

"Anybody that slick looking can't be on the up and up. You go to the movies, and the guy that looks like that is always the villain," he laughed.

"Too bad he's got an alibi," I said. "He was in Salt Lake City at the time Mauston was killed. The police have checked that out."

"I still say it was the Chinese tongs," Bender insisted.

Flegel responded with, "Bolsheviks."

Packard just shrugged. "Say, you aren't going to forget me, are you, Jimmy? You owe me one. If you find out something juicy, tell me about it so the *Chronicle* can get a scoop. Particularly if there's a chance for a nice gruesome photo."

"I'll keep that in mind, Floyd. And thanks for getting me the prints."

On my way out I nodded at the watchman. I don't think he even noticed.

The evening was still young, and the nice weather was still holding, so I headed up to Sutter St. I still had plenty of time to check out the report about Lomax having been spotted at the Hotel Alexandria. If it had been him, he'd been there in the evening, so it made sense to go while there was a good chance that the same staff would be on duty.

10.

Hotel detectives all tend to come out of the same mold. They're older guys with enough beef on them to handle an unruly drunk but not enough left in them to put up a real fight. Most are ex-cops, either retired and trying to make ends meet or else fired for being on the take, or not, as the case may be. Being a hotel dick is a job of last resort for most; the hours are late, the pay is lousy, and respect is nonexistent. It doesn't call for much intelligence, but it does require a certain innate cleverness. The most important skill is an ability to recognize when you're being scammed and when to turn a blind eye.

Gene McCarthy, the detective at the Hotel Alexandria, was typical of the breed. He'd been a cop over in Oakland until he'd gotten into a fracas with a captain that didn't like Irishmen. McCarthy had won the fight but lost his job. I knew him slightly from past cases, and he knew me. In my line, I find it pays to be on reasonably good terms with the hotel detectives around town. Mostly I do that by playing it straight with them and helping them handle any trouble quietly. In McCarthy's case, I'd gotten on his good side by slipping him a pint of Old Overalls once when I'd been running surveillance on someone staying at the Alexandria. That had made me a friend for life.

McCarthy had me spotted as soon as I had come out of the revolving door into the hotel lobby. He caught my eye and then glanced over towards a quiet corner. I took the hint and moseyed over in that direction and sat in one of the chairs. A couple of minutes later McCarthy took an adjacent seat, studiously avoiding eye contact.

"Any trouble I should know about, Tolliver?"

"Nah, nothing like that. I'm just here for some information."

"What kind of information?" McCarthy asked suspiciously.

"I'm just trying to find out if somebody was staying here on a particular date."

"Why are you interested? Did this guy do something wrong?"

"If he did, he didn't do it here. He claims that he was out of town on that particular date, which may be true. The problem is, someone claims to have seen him going into the restaurant here on the night in question. Maybe they were mistaken. They probably were, but I've still got to check it out."

"So what do you want to do?"

"I'd like to check the register for that date."

"If you give me the name I can check it for you. It would be better that way."

"The thing is, if he were in town, chances are he wasn't using his own name."

"Like that, is it?" McCarthy said with a leer. He'd probably figured that I was tracking down an errant husband or wife. I didn't correct him. Nine times out of ten, he would have been right.

"Yeah, if I could get a look at the register for that date I might be able to spot an alias. I've got a picture of him, too, that I'd like to flash around if that won't be a problem?"

I didn't care if it would be a problem or not, but I wanted McCarthy on my side.

"No problem at all. Let's go talk to the desk clerk."

We got up and walked over to the reception desk. The desk clerk was a young kid in his twenties. He looked college educated and bored as hell. He tried to ignore us by fumbling around with some papers behind the counter.

"Mr. McCarthy," the kid said when he realized we weren't going away. "Is there a problem?"

"Francis, this is Mr. Tolliver. He's a private investigator. He's got a few questions he'd like to ask about someone who may have been staying here. He'd like to examine the register."

"I'm not supposed to let anyone see that, Mr. McCarthy. I could get in trouble."

"You could get in trouble for a lot of things, Francis, but not for showing Jim here the book. I promise I won't tell."

I didn't know what McCarthy was alluding to, but it was pretty obvious that the kid did. I could imagine. In a big hotel, there are always lots of ways for a desk clerk to supplement their income.

"Well, if you're sure it's alright, Mr. McCarthy—"

"Sure. I said it was, didn't I. What date did you say you were interested in, Jim?"

"I didn't, but it was August 2nd. He probably stayed only the one night."

The kid got out the register and leafed through the pages until he found the right one, then plopped the book on top of the counter.

I took a look at it, running my finger down the entries. There wasn't any Edward Lomax listed on the page. There was an Edgar Larkin. His address was given as Salt Lake City, and he'd stayed one night. I didn't know that city well enough to tell if the address was legit or not, but I wrote down the information so I could check it later.

"Find what you were looking for, Jim?"

"Maybe." I pulled out the photo I'd gotten of Lomax and showed it to the kid. "Recognize this gentleman by any chance?"

"I don't know. Maybe, maybe not. I see a lot of people, and that was almost a month ago."

"Take another look." This time I helped his memory along with a George Washington.

"Yeah. Maybe. He looks familiar."

"Any chance his name is Edgar Larkin of Salt Lake City?" I pointed at the entry in the register.

He looked at the picture again and then at the register. That seemed to trigger something in his mind. "Yeah, now that I think about it, that's him. Maybe. I guess I'm just not sure."

"That's alright. Like you say, it was a month ago." I couldn't really blame the kid. In a place like the Alexandria, he would have seen hundreds of well-dressed businessmen in August. As an afterthought, I brought out the picture of Mrs. Mauston.

"I don't suppose you remember seeing this woman?"

The kid took a good look at the photograph. I can't say that I blamed him for that, either. It was a good likeness and worth looking at.

"Yeah, I'm pretty sure I've seen her somewhere before."

"Yeah, but was she in the hotel that night?" I pressed.

"Maybe, maybe not. I can't really remember when or where, just that I've seen her."

"Would another buck help you remember?"

"It's not that, Mr. Tolliver, I just don't remember when or where it was."

"Okay. Forget about that. Let's get back to this Edgar Larkin. What do you remember about him? Was he alone? Did he have a woman with him?"

"This is a respectable hotel, Mr. Tolliver," the kid said indignantly. I could see the smirk on McCarthy's face.

"Yeah. Respectable and discrete."

"He was alone when he checked in. But I noticed as he walked away that there was a lady that seemed to be waiting for him."

"Any chance it was the lady in the picture?"

"I couldn't see her face. She was facing the other way."

"But did she look like she might be the same woman? From the back, I mean?"

"Well, she was attractive from that angle—if you know what I mean—" That seemed to embarrass the kid. McCarthy snickered.

"Did you see where they went? Did they go up to his room?"

"No. I didn't. Another guest came to the desk right then, and when I looked up, they were both gone."

"You don't happen to remember what time this all happened, do you?"

"I don't know. Seven-thirty or eight I guess."

"Thanks, you've been a big help." The kid beamed like a golden retriever that's been patted on the head. I slipped him another buck.

McCarthy and I wandered away from the desk. "Let me take a look at them pictures of yours, Tolliver."

I handed them over. McCarthy took a good long look.

"Have you seen either one of them before."

"Sure, but I'm not sure where. I don't think it was in the hotel, though. Was there anyone else you'd like to talk to?"

"Yeah. The maitre d' in the restaurant if he's the same one that was on duty the second."

"That'll be Luigi. He works pretty near every night, so chances are good he was working that night."

We headed over to the doorway leading into the restaurant. Luigi proved to be a little bald Italian guy with a big mustache and a bigger smile.

"Howdy, Mr. McCarthy. You want a table? I gotta nice one just for you and your friend."

"No thanks. We just need a little info. Mr. Tolliver here would like to ask you a few questions."

"Sure thing. Ask away."

I hauled out the photos again and showed them to Luigi. "Have you seen either of these people in the restaurant? It would have been about a month ago, around the start of August?"

Luigi pulled a pair of spectacles out of his inside jacket pocket and perched them on his nose. He gave the photographs a good examination, particularly that of Mrs. Mauston.

"Nice lookin' woman, but I don't remember seeing her. I'd remember, too. I always remember the ladies. But the gentleman. He looks familiar. Yeah, I think he came into the restaurant one night, maybe back when you asked about."

"Was he with anyone?"

"No, he came in alone. That's why I remember him. A nice looking guy like that eating alone—"

"But the woman wasn't with him?"

"No. I would have remembered. Just the gentleman. It was late, too. Almost at closing."

"When would that be?"

"We close at midnight, but I don't like to seat people after ten-thirty, eleven."

"But the gentleman came in alone around eleven or so?"

"A little earlier, maybe ten-fifteen. He had a beef steak and a salad. And a glass of wine. No dessert."

"I don't suppose you remember which night this was?"

Luigi just shrugged.

"Thanks, you've been a big help." I slipped him a couple of bucks. Luigi just smiled.

"You've been pretty free with the money, Tolliver," McCarthy commented.

"I'm getting expenses."

"So what gives? This seems like it's more than just a cheating spouse."

"Yeah, maybe. It's just that this Edgar Larkin ain't Edgar Larkin, and he claims he was somewhere other than San Francisco the night of August the second. I find that interesting."

McCarthy thought about that a bit. Then it was like a light going on in his head.

"I know where I seen those two before. It was in the *Chronicle*. Their pictures were together. Something about the dame's husband having committed suicide. Say, you don't think that the wife and this Larkin character, or whoever he is, were having an affair or something and that's why her old man croaked himself, do you?"

"No, I don't think that's what happened at all," I replied honestly. "But I find it curious that this Larkin character was in San Francisco that night when he told the police he was in Salt Lake City."

It dawned on McCarthy what the implications were. "Say, you don't think—"

"I don't think anything for the moment."

"But shouldn't we be going to the cops?"

"I'd prefer not to, for the moment. After all, we don't have proof of much of anything, just a name in a register and a couple of people who saw someone who may or may not be Edgar Larkin, and one person who saw a woman who from the back maybe looked like the widow, and maybe went up to a man's room of an evening. I'll let you in on a secret, McCarthy. Mrs. Mauston is the one who hired me. She's trying to prove that her husband was murdered. I'd just as soon her name stayed out of the papers, at least until I'm sure of what's going on. I suspect the hotel would be just as happy to avoid having a scandal associated with it."

"Yeah, I guess you're right, Tolliver."

"I appreciate your help, tonight, McCarthy," I said as I shook his hand. I slipped him a sawbuck at the same time. "Let's just keep things on the Q.T. I'll notify the police if and when I think it appropriate."

McCarthy gave me a wink and walked me to the hotel entrance. Out in the cool night air, I wondered what it all meant.

It was still early, and I had one more thing to do. I caught a cab outside the hotel and told the driver to take me to the Ferry Building. From there, I took the ferry across to the Oakland Pier station. I could have saved myself some time by using the telephone, but I've found I usually have more luck getting the information I need face to face. Besides, the time spent on the boat staring at the waters of the East Bay was time that I could use thinking. I figured that I could use it.

Lomax had said that he had taken the sleeper train from Salt Lake City the day after Mauston's death. I knew that Miller had verified that fact, but I wanted to look into it myself. If Edgar Larkin had really been Lomax, then his alibi had as many holes as Swiss cheese, but so far I didn't have anything I could hang him with.

The station master, when I tracked him down in his office was helpful. I think he thought I was with the insurance company. I didn't try to persuade him otherwise.

"Sure, I know which train you're talking about. The police were already here asking me about it."

"So you're sure that Lomax was on the train that arrived from Salt Lake City on the morning of the sixth of August."

"Sure as I can be. I've got the passenger list right here." He dug through some papers on his desk and came up with the manifest. "See, Edward Lomax, sleeping compartment 3."

"And you're sure he was in that compartment."

"That car was fully booked, and there was a waiting list for sleeping compartments. If he hadn't showed up for the train, someone else would have gotten the compartment."

"I guess that settles that, then. You've been a big help. Say, is there any chance I could talk to the attendant or whatever that was manning the sleeper car that night?"

"Let's see." He consulted another list. "That would be Sam Pickins. I'm afraid you can't talk to him right now, Mr. Tolliver. He's out working on a train. In fact, right now he's on the night train from Salt Lake City. But if you come around in the morning, say about eight, you should be able to catch him."

"Thanks. That would be swell. I'll be back."

"I'm always ready to help the authorities."

I said my goodbyes and took the ferry back to San Francisco. It was late, and I'd done enough legwork for one day.

11.

I was down at the Ferry Building at eight o'clock sharp to take the boat over to the Oakland Pier where the Southern Pacific trains disembarked. I'd had a couple of eggs over easy with bacon and a cup of coffee and was feeling pretty chipper. Once in the station, I looked at the arrivals board and found out which track the overnight from Salt Lake City was on.

Sam Pickins, when I found him, proved to be a slender Negro around fifty years old. He had tired eyes but a big smile, though I couldn't tell if the latter was genuine or just part of the uniform. He was friendly enough when I introduced myself and friendlier still after I had slipped him a couple of bucks.

"Mr. Lomax. Sure I remember him. He was the man the police were here asking about." He pronounced police as two words, "po" and "leese."

"Yes, that's him, Sam. You told the police that he was on your car that night."

"Yes, sir. Compartment 3."

"I've got a picture here. I'd like to have you look at it and tell me if it's of the man that was in compartment 3." I showed him the picture. He took a good look at it and then handed it back.

"That's him, sho' enough. I've got a good memory for faces, you have to in this line of work, and that's the gentleman that was in compartment 3. Nice gentleman, too. Gave me a good tip. Not all of them do, you know."

"I can imagine," I said sympathetically. "So you couldn't be mistaken?"

"No, sir," he said emphatically.

I have to admit I was disappointed. I'd been trying to build up a scenario that had Lomax in San Francisco the night Mauston died, but Sam's testimony would seem to rule that out.

"Well, thanks, Sam. You've been helpful."

I was about to leave when the attendant said, "Funny thing about it though—"

"What's funny about it Sam?"

"Well, it's like this, Mr. Tolliver. You see, I work the trains to Salt Lake City and back again. One night out to Salt Lake City and then the next night I work the train back. I get a day off, and then I do it all over again, with two days off on Saturday and Sunday."

I could see that Sam had a story to tell, but that I was going to have to let him tell it his own way and in his own time.

"Sounds like a lot of long hours," I said to encourage him.

"Oh, it ain't so bad, Mr. Tolliver. Like I said, I get Wednesdays off and the weekends, Of course, the days I do work I put in a good twelve hours if you include getting the car ready and cleaning up after we're done. But working for the railroad is good steady work, so I ain't got no complaints."

"You've got to look on the bright side—"

"Sho' enough."

"But you said there was something funny having to do with Mr. Lomax?"

"Yes. That's the part I was getting to. Like I said, I worked the train to Salt Lake City the night before the one you were askin' about. It left San Francisco just after midnight and got into Salt Lake City the morning of the third. The day before the other one."

"Right." I was getting a little impatient, but I could tell Sam was building up to something, something that he thought would be a bombshell.

"So, I was working the car, and one of the passengers asked me to get him a nightcap. A whiskey and soda. So I went to the club car and got the bartender there to mix the drink so I could take it back. Well, on my way back, that's when I saw him. Sitting in the club car having a drink. Of course, I didn't think anything of it at the time. No reason to. But like I tol' you, I've got a good memory for faces. That's why I thought it was funny."

"Wait a minute, Sam. You've lost me. Who did you see? Who was the man in the club car?"

"That's what I'm trying to tell you, Mr. Tolliver. It was that Mr. Lomax. The gentleman in the photograph you jus' showed me. The one who was in compartment three the next night. That's why I thought it was funny. Why take all the trouble to go to Salt Lake City only to come back on the train the next night. Why he couldn't have had more than fourteen or fifteen hours in Salt Lake City between trains."

"And you're sure it was Lomax?"

"Well, I didn't know it at the time, of course. He wasn't in my car that night, so I didn't know his name. But I recognized him the next night when I got his compartment ready for him. It was the same man, right enough. Like I said, I've got a good memory for faces. You've got to in this job."

"I'm sure you do, Sam. One more thing, what time did the train leave that night, the one to Salt Lake City?"

"Why it left right on time. Twelve-fifteen."

"Thanks, Sam. Just out of curiosity, why didn't you tell this to the police?"

"Well, they didn't ask. They just wanted to know if he was on the train from Salt Lake City. They didn't ask no questions about the train the night before."

Looking at it from Sam's viewpoint I could understand the logic. A man in his position doesn't volunteer information to the police. Not if he can help it.

"Sam, why are you telling this to me instead of the police?"

"Well, like I said, the police didn't ask. They didn't give me no two bucks, either, Mr. Tolliver."

"No, I'm sure they didn't, Sam," I said with a grin. I pulled out my wallet and slipped Sam a fin. His grin was bigger than ever, and this time I was sure it was genuine.

"Thanks again, Sam."

"You got any more questions, Mr. Tolliver, you know where to find me."

"I'll keep that in mind, Sam."

After I left Sam, I hunted up the station master. There was a different man on during the day shift, but he was just as helpful when I showed him my credentials. He got the passenger list for the night train to Salt Lake City. There wasn't any Edward Lomax on it. There was, however, an Edgar Larkin who had booked a coach seat. I thanked the station master after assuring him that he'd been helpful and headed back to the office.

I had a lot to think about on the ferry back across the bay. It was pretty clear now that Lomax had been in San Francisco the night Mauston had been killed. Not only that, but he'd lied about the fact, both to me and to the police. The question was, why had he lied and what had he been up to? I still had nothing to tie him directly to Mauston's murder. There were a couple of things that didn't quite jibe, as well. If Lomax had eaten dinner at the Alexandria at around ten-fifteen or ten-thirty, and then caught the train to Salt Lake a little after midnight, would he have had the time to go to the offices of Far Eastern and shoot Mauston? Allowing forty-five minutes for his dinner, he'd have left the hotel at a little after eleven. From the hotel, a cab to the Ferry Building would have taken maybe ten minutes or less. The ferries left on the half-hour and the ride to the railroad pier in Oakland was about half an hour. Sam had said the train left on time at twelve-fifteen. If Lomax planned Mauston's murder beforehand, and that was pretty much the only explanation for his having made the trip from Salt Lake City, he'd been cutting things pretty fine as far as the timing went. It might just be possible, but it would have been cutting it close.

The smart thing to do at that point would have been to drop this new information in Lt. Miller's lap and let him worry about the details, but then I've never been known for doing the smart thing. I decided to sit on what I knew and maybe have a chat with Lomax about it before I went to the police.

I was still distracted by this question when I got back to my office, which was why I didn't notice the man sitting on the bench in the hallway until I had the key inserted in the door. It was the insurance salesman that I'd been seeing around.

"Could I have a word with you, Mr. Tolliver?"

"I'm not interested in any insurance if that's what you're selling."

"Oh, I'm not here to sell you insurance, Mr. Tolliver, but I do work for an insurance company."

He reached inside his jacket. I tensed for a moment, but then realized he was only pulling out a business card and not a pistol.

I took the card. It identified the salesman as a Jakob Mandelbrot, Special Investigator for the Western National Insurance Company. I gave Mandlebrot the once over. He didn't look much like a special investigator, but then that was probably to his advantage. I couldn't see the telltale bulge of a pistol, either, but maybe he wasn't that kind of investigator. I pocketed the card.

I finished unlocking the office door. "Why don't we step inside?"

Once inside I said, "Have a seat, Mr. Mandelbrot," waving in the direction of the chair facing the desk, the same chair Mrs. Mauston had sat in.

He took the seat, setting his briefcase down gently on the floor next to the chair. He gave a quick glance around the office, the same kind of glance that a policeman instinctively gives to every room he enters. I have no doubt he would be able to recall later every detail down to the picture on the wall calendar.

"What can I do for you, Mr. Mandelbrot?"

"I understand that you're working for Helen Mauston." It was more of a statement than a question. I wasn't sure where he'd gotten the information. It didn't really matter.

"What if I am?"

"Oh, nothing, really. Mrs. Mauston, of course, has every right to hire an investigator. I am just curious as to why."

"And you chose to satisfy your curiosity by asking me. Maybe you should be asking Mrs. Mauston that question, though I suspect that an insurance policy worth two-hundred and fifty G.'s has something to do with it. Of course, you'd know all about that policy, wouldn't you, Mr. Mandelbrot?"

"You state the obvious, Mr. Tolliver."

"Let's quit fencing, shall we. I'm trying to prove that Mauston was murdered. You're trying to prove that he killed himself. It would seem that we are working at cross purposes, Mr. Mandelbrot. I'm not sure what business we have with each other. If, and when, I find something relevant to the case, I'll present it to the police. Until such time, I'll keep the details of my investigation to myself."

"I understand, Mr. Tolliver. That is, of course, the *ethical* thing to do." I didn't particularly like the way he said ethical, but I wasn't going to let him get my goat.

"You realize, of course, Mr. Tolliver, that there is another reason besides suicide that would relieve Western National of the necessity of having to pay out on the policy?"

"And what would that be?"

"If it were to be proven that the beneficiary was responsible for the death of the insured."

"Look here, Mr. Mandelbrot, if you're implying that my client was in any way responsible—"

"Oh, I'm not implying anything, Mr. Tolliver," Mandelbrot interrupted. "I was just making a simple statement of fact. I should also add, that if that were to be the case, Western National might be generous, within reason, to whoever was able to prove it."

"Look, you little—If my client had anything to do with her husband's death, why would she have hired an investigator to prove that it was murder?"

"Why, indeed, Mr. Tolliver? Maybe *that's* the question you should be asking yourself."

"Just why have you been following me around, Mandelbrot. And what are you doing here? Are you trying to warn me off, or are you just trying to annoy me?"

"Neither, actually, Mr. Tolliver. I was just curious to see what type of man you were."

"And have you figured that out?"

"Not yet. You're proving to be more complex than I had originally assumed. Perhaps Mrs. Mauston made a mistake when she hired you."

"Look, I'm going to get to the bottom of this mess, one way or another, and nothing you can do will stop me."

"Yes. That's exactly what I mean."

Despite my intentions, I was starting to get annoyed with Mandelbrot.

"Unless you've got something more to say besides riddles—"

"No. Nothing for the present. But keep my card, Mr. Tolliver. You might find yourself wanting to follow up on my suggestion."

With that, Mandelbrot picked up his briefcase and left.

12.

I wasn't sure what the insurance man had meant by his remarks. Frankly, I wasn't sure about anything anymore, but the insurance man had gotten under my skin. His crack about ethics and what that implied—well, I didn't like what it implied.

I wasn't sure what game Mandelbrot was playing, but I was sure that he was playing some game. Of course, it was possible that he'd been telling the truth. People do that—sometimes. If he did work for the insurance company, and all I had for proof of that was a cheap business card and his word, it would certainly be to his advantage to have the murder pinned on Mrs. Mauston. He might not get a percentage, but his bosses would certainly look kindly on his having saved them a quarter-of-a-million dollars. Even establishing some level of doubt might enable the company to reduce the amount of any eventual settlement.

But what if the other possibility was true? What if Mandelbrot didn't work for Western National? What game could he be playing then? Blackmail? It was a possibility. He certainly seemed to know a lot about the case. It was possible that he had information that could in some way implicate Mrs. Mauston in her husband's death, or at least raise embarrassing questions. More importantly, he might know something that would allow the insurance company to refuse to pay out on the policy. Had his approaching me been an overture of sorts, the opening gambit in a play for a portion of the quarter-million? Was he just being cagey by dealing with me instead of dealing with Mrs. Mauston directly?

I didn't have any answers to these questions, but I thought it might be worth my while trying to get them. I might as well. I wasn't getting anywhere with the murder. I had wanted to talk to Lomax again and confront him about the Hotel Alexandria, but he wasn't at Far Eastern, nor had he answered when I had called his home. With that part of the case on hold, it might make sense to look into Mandelbrot.

The card Mandelbrot had left me gave the address of Western National as being on Powell Street. I recognized the number as that of an office building. A quick check of the city directory confirmed the fact. There was only one Mandelbrot listed in the phone book, at 811 Geary, which if I remembered rightly, was an apartment building. I decided that maybe it was time to give Mandelbrot a taste of his own medicine.

I got up early the next morning, and by seven I had found a place across the street from where I could observe the entrance to 811 Geary. I hadn't bothered with any of sort of disguise. You only find that kind of thing in mystery stories. Nothing makes a man stand out more than a fake mustache or beard. Instead, I was dressed in my second best suit and a perfectly respectable snap-brimmed hat.

At just after eight Mandelbrot walked out of the building's door. He was wearing a brown suit, carried a briefcase and looked no different than dozens of other men going to work. He turned the corner onto Post and walked briskly down the street for two blocks. He entered a diner on the corner and took a stool at the counter. From what I could see through the plate glass window of the diner, he was greeted as a regular by the waitress. He probably ate breakfast there every day of the week.

I wandered into the drugstore across the street and pretended an interest in a rack of detective magazines. After allowing Mandelbrot fifteen minutes for his breakfast, I grabbed one of the magazines at random and paid for it at the counter. Outside on the street, I stood on the corner thumbing through it in an absentminded manner until Mandelbrot came out of the diner, then I tossed it in a trash bin and followed after him as he continued up Post.

At Powell, he grabbed a cable car headed north. I didn't make any effort to catch the car because I had a good idea of where he was headed. Instead, I caught the next car headed in that direction.

I got off the car a few blocks up and entered the building where Western National had their offices. I'd guessed right because just as I walked into the lobby, I saw Mandelbrot enter an elevator. A quick glance at the directory next to the elevators confirmed the insurance company had offices on the sixth floor. Satisfied, I bought a paper at the newsstand and then grabbed a seat in the lobby coffee shop where I could keep an eye on the elevators.

The waitress behind the counter was a skinny twenty-year-old with limp light brown hair framing a face that might have been pretty if she didn't look so tired. When she came to take my order, I said, "I'll take a cup of coffee and one of those glazed donuts." I hadn't had breakfast, and tailing Mandelbrot, it wasn't clear when I'd have a chance to grab a meal.

When the coffee came, it was weaker than I liked it, but adding sugar or cream would have just diluted it. The donut wasn't bad. I took my time with both and pretended to read the paper that I had set out in front of me. I was just at the point where I'd have to order another cup of coffee to avoid attracting attention when Mandelbrot popped out of the elevator. I left change on the counter to cover the coffee and donut and give the waitress a dime tip but picked up the paper in case I needed it for cover.

Outside, I spotted Mandelbrot heading down Powell. I followed about a block behind. Fortunately, it appeared Mandelbrot liked to get his exercise. It's a lot easier to follow someone on foot than it is in a cab despite what you see in the movies. He walked down Powell all the way to Market and then turned right. He crossed over Market a couple of blocks further down and continued south for a couple of blocks more.

There was a pumper truck parked in the street, and a couple of firemen were rolling up some hoses. The street had been barricaded, and I joined the row of gawkers behind them. Mandelbrot said something to the cop keeping people back, and he let the insurance man through.

I asked one of the bystanders what had happened, and he told me there had been a fire in an Italian restaurant. It had happened in the middle of the night, and as far as he knew, nobody had been hurt.

A guy I recognized as a detective with the fire department's arson squad came out of the building as Mandelbrot approached. I couldn't overhear what they were saying, but from the way they shook hands and chatted, they were well acquainted with each other. The two of them went back inside the restaurant.

I stood around for a half an hour or so watching the fire truck pack up and get ready to leave. The crowd of gawkers thinned out as it became obvious the show was over. Finally, Mandelbrot came out, shook the arson man's hand again and headed back towards Market. I followed after.

Either Mandelbrot really was an investigator for the insurance company, or he was playing one of the most elaborate cons I'd ever seen. I was almost ready to call it quits, but I'd invested enough time to make me want to carry it through.

It looked like Mandelbrot was going to catch a cable car back up Powell at the Market Street turntable, but as I came up on it, I saw him slip away from the waiting passengers and head up Eddy. I wondered if he had spotted me. I sprinted after him just in time to see him turn onto Mason. As I turned the corner to follow, I found myself face to face with the insurance man.

"You've been following me all morning, Mr. Tolliver," Mandelbrot said. His sounded more amused than angry.

"I thought it only fair, Mandelbrot. After all, turnabout is fair play."

"Touché, Mr. Tolliver. Did you find out what you were interested in?"

"Oh, I think I've got a pretty good idea, now."

"And just what *were* you trying to discover, Mr. Tolliver?"

"Oh, I wondered just what kind of man you were."

"And just what kind of man am I?" he asked.

"The kind that eats breakfast in the same diner every morning, that likes exercise, and who takes his job seriously."

"I could have told you that if you'd asked, Mr. Tolliver."

"Yeah, but I might not have believed you."

"No, I suppose you wouldn't have. In your place, I probably wouldn't have, either. Are you satisfied?"

"For the moment."

"Then I suggest both our times would be better spent trying to find out who was responsible for Mauston's death."

"Then you *do* think it was murder?" I asked.

"I think that it's likely, Mr. Tolliver. Don't you?"

"You're probably right," I agreed. "Just out of curiosity, was that restaurant fire arson?"

Mandelbrot looked at me a little surprised. At first, I thought he was going to refuse to answer, but then he changed his mind.

"No, it wasn't arson. It was just a kitchen fire. They hadn't cleaned the grease trap recently. You'll find that most restaurant fires are due to carelessness on the part of the kitchen staff."

I was almost disappointed.

"Well, good morning."

"Good morning, Mr. Tolliver. And remember what I said about letting me know if you find out who killed Charles Mauston."

"I'll keep that in mind."

"You do that," Mandelbrot said, walking off with a cheery wave.

On my way back to the office, I considered the morning's work. I'd had my bit of fun with the insurance man. While following him, I hadn't made any great effort to hide the fact, but still, he'd had me spotted almost from the beginning. There was no question that he was an experienced operative and a sharp one, too. There didn't seem to be much question that he was exactly what he claimed to be, an investigator for the insurance company. Either that or he was working an extremely elaborate con; though, for a quarter-of-a-million, that couldn't be completely ruled out. Granting, though, that he was an insurance investigator, that didn't necessarily rule out that he was playing some game of his own, even if I couldn't figure out what it was.

Whatever the case, we'd laid our cards on the table for each other, and it was time for me to get back to work.

13.

Frankly, even if I ignored Mandelbrot, I wasn't sure about anything anymore. It was pretty clear that Lomax had lied about being in Salt Lake City. He'd been in San Francisco that night. But what had he been doing there? If I could trust the witnesses at the Hotel Alexandria, and none of them had had any reason to lie, then he wouldn't have had time to kill Mauston and still catch the night train back to Salt Lake City. But, if he hadn't killed Mauston, why had he lied about being in San Francisco that night? Why had he tried so hard to establish an alibi?

It didn't make sense, and the only way I could see to make sense out of it was to confront Lomax with the fact that his alibi was phony and see what he'd have to say for himself.

I placed a call to Far Eastern Specialties. Lomax wasn't in. I asked to speak to the office manager, Nilgren, and the woman who had answered the phone connected me.

"Thomas Nilgren speaking."

"This is James Tolliver. I was there the other day."

"Yes, the detective. I remember. What can I do for you, Mr. Tolliver?"

"I'd like to talk to Mr. Lomax. There are a few points that I want to clarify."

"I'm afraid Mr. Lomax isn't here right now."

"When will he be back?"

"I'm not quite sure, Mr. Tolliver. Mr. Lomax didn't say."

"Well, did he leave word where he could be reached? This is important."

"No, I'm afraid he didn't. I got the impression that he was going out of town for a few days."

"Isn't it a little bit irregular for the sole remaining partner to be absent without leaving word about where he can be reached?"

There was a moment of silence as Nilgren thought that over. When he spoke again, there was a note of exasperation in his voice.

"I'm afraid, Mr. Tolliver, that things have been very irregular here since Mr. Mauston died. Mr. Mauston was responsible for all of the day-to-day operations. Now that Mr. Lomax is in charge, well, he hasn't been keen on following through with things in a timely manner. I'm afraid it's made things most difficult for the staff."

"I'm sure it has, Mr. Nilgren," I said, trying to placate the manager. "If Mr. Lomax should get in touch with you, will you ask him to give me a call? Tell him that's it's very important, for him as much as for me."

"Of course, Mr. Tolliver," Nilgren answered, almost sounding glad to have a definite order. I gave him my office and home phone numbers and hung up.

It occurred to me that someone in the shop might have an idea of where Lomax was. I looked up the number in the directory and called. The voice that answered that answered was smooth and cool as silk.

"Far Eastern Specialties. Miss Bouchet speaking. How may I help you?"

"Miss Bouchet? This is James Tolliver. I don't know if you remember me—"

"Of course I remember you, Mr. Tolliver. What may I do for you?" I had the impression that she was being careful of what she said because someone in the shop might overhear.

"I'm trying to locate Mr. Lomax. They don't seem to know where he is, in the office. I was hoping that someone in the shop might have an idea where I could find him."

"I'm afraid I can't help you, Mr. Tolliver. I don't know where he is. Mr. Lomax didn't inform us of his plans." She had started out sounding a little snippy, but then she realized she didn't want to take her frustrations out on me.

"Perhaps I could ask you a few questions, then."

"I'm afraid I'm busy with a customer right at the moment, Mr. Tolliver."

"Perhaps I could stop by later, then."

There was a pause, then she said, "I have a better idea, Mr. Tolliver. Why don't we meet for dinner? I'll be free, then, to give you my undivided attention."

"That would be wonderful, Miss Bouchet. Where shall I pick you up?"

"Why don't we meet at the restaurant, instead? Are you familiar with Le Maison Saigon?"

"I'm sure I can find it."

"Shall we say, seven-thirty, then?"

"Seven-thirty it is."

"Until then, Mr. Tolliver. Good-bye."

The line went dead before I could reply. I wasn't quite sure what to think. Miss Bouchet, however beautiful she might be, had struck me as the prim and proper type. Despite that, she had proved to be a fast worker. Unless, that is, she had something other than a free meal on her mind. Either way, it might prove to be an interesting evening.

Le Maison Saigon was located on the respectable fringe of Chinatown. I hadn't been sure what to expect, but the restaurant displayed none of the usual oriental trappings of your typical Chinese place, but then Saigon was in French Indochina. Occupying a small storefront, with white half-curtains in the plate glass windows and an overhead awning, it would not have looked out of place on a Parisian boulevard. The waiter in a short, black jacket standing in the doorway would have completed the impression if he had looked even remotely French.

When I approached, the waiter asked, "Mr. Tolliver?"

"That's me."

"If you'll come this way?" The waiter's accent was reminiscent of Miss Bouchet's.

I was led to a small booth at the rear of the restaurant where Miss Bouchet was waiting. She looked nothing like the prim saleswoman I remembered. Her black hair curled softly around shoulders bared by the evening dress she wore, a dress of a pale rose color that complemented her skin perfectly. I was glad that I had decided to wear my best suit.

"Mr. Tolliver," she greeted me as I sat down.

"Miss Bouchet. May I say you look lovely tonight."

"I get so few chances to dine out. I thought I'd take advantage of the occasion."

"I find that hard to believe, Miss Bouchet."

"Oh, I live a most sheltered life, Mr. Tolliver."

"It seems a shame to ruin things by being so formal. You can call me Jim, or James if you prefer."

"James. I like that. It suits you."

"And may I call you—"

"Please. Not Flo," she protested.

"No, I can see how that wouldn't work. Florence, then."

"As you wish, James," she replied demurely.

The waiter interrupted this banter to bring us menus. They were in French. From what I could read, so was the cuisine.

"Do you read French, James?"

"Some. I picked it up during the war. I can usually make myself understood, as long as the topic of conversation is simple."

"I'll translate for you if you need."

"I admit that I'm a little confused," I waved a hand around the restaurant.

"Saigon, that's where I grew up, James, is a very cosmopolitan city where French, Chinese, and Indochinese influences rub shoulders. I like this place because it reminds me of home."

"I see," I said awkwardly. "If you don't mind my asking, how did you come to be living in San Francisco?"

"As I told you earlier, I grew up in Saigon. My father was French; my mother was Chinese. Both families were against the marriage, but I believe my parents were very much in love. Unfortunately, my mother died when I was quite young, so I was raised by my father as quite French. I was educated at a convent school in Saigon, a quite good education, really, for a French woman. Then my father died when I was eighteen. I was left alone. My mother's family had never really accepted my parent's marriage or me. I'm not sure what would have happened without Mr. Mauston."

"So you knew him back then?" I asked, eager to find out more about Mauston's background.

"He knew my father. They had been business associates and friends. When he learned of my father's death, he arranged for me to come to America and offered me a position in the shop. He was very kind and generous. I've worked there ever since."

I didn't quite know how to fit this in with the image I had built of Charles Mauston. He hadn't struck me as overly charitable or kind, but then most of what I knew about him had come from the papers.

We were interrupted at that point by waiter coming to take our orders. I had the steak au poivre; she had something with chicken. I'm not sure what. She suggested a bottle of wine. Me, I'm more of a rye man, so I let her choose. There followed an extended conversation with the waiter after which a bottle appeared.

"We've talked enough about myself, James. What about you? How did you become a private detective? And how did *you* end up in San Francisco?"

"Me. There's not a lot to tell."

"But you were in the war? In France?"

"Briefly. Right at the end. Not in the trenches, though, thank God. For some reason, they stuck me in Intelligence. Probably because I could speak a little German. After the war, I needed a job. The Continental Agency was hiring, so I got on with them. That's how I ended up in San Francisco. They needed operatives on the west coast, so they sent me here. I liked the climate, so I've stayed."

"In San Francisco? With the fogs?" Florence remarked incredulously.

"No snow. That's the part that I like."

"So you came to San Francisco. But you don't work for the Continental Agency anymore, do you?"

"No I decided I preferred being my own boss, so I opened up my own agency. It's pretty much a one-man operation, but I get by."

"That must be nice, being your own boss, being in control of your own destiny."

"It has its good points."

"And it's bad ones?"

"I'm living pretty much hand to mouth at times."

"Still—" There was a note of wistfulness in her voice.

The waiter brought our food, and for a while, we ate and made small talk. We avoided the subject of Mauston and our past lives.

After we had finished our dinner, the waiter served coffee.

"This has been nice, James, but you didn't ask me to dinner just for the pleasure of my company—"

"As I remember it, you were the one who asked me to dinner."

She smiled at that, then said, "Seriously, James, you said you had some questions—"

"Yes. I've got plenty of questions, though I don't know if you can answer any of them."

"Then you believe that Mr. Mauston was murdered?"

"Oh, he was murdered, alright. I'm just not sure by who."

"But you think you have an idea of who it was, don't you?"

"I'm pretty sure it was one of two people. Or maybe the two of them working together. But things just don't add up. I'm hoping to fill in some of the blanks."

"And those blanks are—?"

"For one, Lomax's alibi about being in Salt Lake City doesn't wash. I've got witnesses who can put him here in San Francisco that night. I want to know what he was doing. That's why I've been looking for him. But he seems to have done a bunk."

"You think that Mr. Lomax killed Mr. Mauston?"

"That's just it. I don't. Oh, he was in San Francisco that night, and he lied about the fact to the police. That's certainly suspicious. But I've also got witnesses that say he was on a train headed to Salt Lake City that left shortly after midnight.

According to the Medical Examiner Mauston wasn't killed until sometime after midnight. If Lomax was on that train, then he couldn't be the one that killed Mauston. But if Lomax didn't kill Mauston, why has he been lying?"

"And how do you think I can help you?"

"I don't know. Maybe you can't." I hesitated for a moment then asked, "Just how well do you know Lomax?"

"As I told you earlier, not very well."

"I know that's what you said earlier. But you didn't know me then, and I didn't know you. From what I've seen, Lomax fancies himself as something of a lady's man. Don't tell me that he never made advances in your direction."

"I won't tell you that, because it wouldn't be true. But they never went anywhere because Mr. Mauston put a stop to it. He said that he'd dissolve the partnership if Lomax didn't leave me alone."

"And did he?"

"He did. He needed the money. Besides, he had plenty of other women available to him. He didn't need me."

"I see. One of these other women wouldn't happen to have been Mrs. Mauston, would she?"

"I don't know, James. It's possible, I suppose. Maybe even likely, but I don't move in those social circles."

I looked deeply into her dark eyes. I thought she was telling the truth—about that, but there was something else that she wanted to get off her very lovely chest.

"James, I have a confession to make."

14.

I looked across the table at my companion. She was anything but the inscrutable oriental at that moment. There was something on her mind, something serious.

"You aren't going to tell me that you are the one who killed Charles Mauston, are you? If you are, that's something more properly to be told to the police."

She looked surprised for a moment, as if the idea that she might be considered a suspect had never even entered her mind.

"No, I didn't kill Charles, and I don't know who did, James." I noted that she had said Charles and not Mr. Mauston. I didn't remember her ever having used his Christian name before, and she had said it in the way a woman says the name of a man that she is close to.

"I didn't ever think you had, Florence, but I'm glad to hear you say it. I'd like to add that I believe you."

She smiled a smile like the Mona Lisa. "I'm glad you believe me, but there's something I want you to know, James. It will probably come out eventually, but I want you to hear it first from me."

"If it isn't pertinent to my investigation, you don't have to tell me anything you don't want to."

"But I do want to, James. You deserve to know."

She had me worried. Until that moment, the night had been going swimmingly, one of the best nights that I'd had in a long time. And now I had a feeling that it was all going to come crashing down around us.

"Alright, go ahead."

"There's no easy way to say this, so I'm just going to say it. I was Charles Mauston's mistress."

I think I must have been expecting something worse. I'm not one of those men who expects every woman to be a virgin, especially when they are young, attractive, and very desirable. All the same, though, her having said it had suddenly turned our relationship, what there was of it, professional.

"You really don't need to tell me anything more, Miss Bouchet. It's none of my business."

"I thought we had agreed that you would call me Florence?"

"That was when we were having a nice dinner. Now, this is business. I'm not the police, Miss Bouchet, but you need to know that anything you say I may use against you."

"I see. But a moment ago you said that you believed me when I said that I hadn't killed Charles."

"And I still do. But it's not what I believe that matters. It's what I can prove."

She looked me deep in the eyes. Not many women can do that, not really. "Yes, I can see that. That's why I'm going to tell you everything, James. You need to know."

"Okay. I'll listen, and if I don't think it has any bearing on the case, I won't ever tell anyone else."

"I told you that when my father died Charles came to Saigon and arranged for me to come to San Francisco. That wasn't such an easy thing to do, my mother not being European. But Charles knew the right people and the right things to put down in the forms, that kind of thing. On my papers, it says that I'm a French citizen, which of course I am, but Charles knew that if I entered through an eastern port such as New Orleans, that fewer questions would be asked, so that's what he arranged. I won't bore you with the details, but they involved a long sea voyage on a somewhat disreputable steamer. It wasn't bad. Actually, the captain spoke decent French and owed Charles a favor.

"Anyway, I arrived in America, took a train to San Francisco, where Charles gave me a job in his shop. I didn't mind. It's interesting work. I've learned a lot about oriental art and antiquities. And it pays well. At least more than most women my age make. So you can see that I owed Charles a great deal. If it hadn't been for him, I don't know what would have become of me, though I think we can both imagine."

She gave a little shudder. I wanted to reach across the table and put my hand on hers. I didn't.

"I try not to make judgments about people, Miss Bouchet."

"But as a detective, don't you have to?"

"That's different. That's about what people do, or have done, not about why they did them."

"I'm not sure that I see the difference."

"There is one, though it's something that's hard to explain. But that's not important now. When you came to America, did you have an—arrangement with Mr. Mauston?"

"You mean to be his mistress? No, that wasn't part of the arrangement. I was just a young girl then, scarcely twenty. I worked in the shop learning about antiques. I was good with the customers, and growing up in Saigon I was good with languages, French, Chinese, even a little Japanese. My English, of course, got much better quickly. I have to say that I was quite happy with the way things were. But at first, no, I wasn't Charles' mistress."

She took a sip of what was left of her wine.

"Charles was like an uncle. Kind, helpful. He had just met Helen then. He was infatuated with her. She's that kind of woman. She can make men think that they love her, even when they don't. They were married shortly after I came to San Francisco. At first, everything seemed to be fine with their marriage, but after a while, I think the bloom had worn off. I could tell that Charles wasn't particularly happy. I was sad for him. He'd been so kind and generous to me—"

She paused for a moment. I didn't say anything. This was her story, and it would be best if she told it in her own way.

"Charles used to take me to dinner, sometimes, just the two of us. Especially if he was planning to work late. We'd talk about my father and the old days in Saigon. He'd ask me how I was getting on in the shop, things like that. All very innocent. But one night, after things had started to sour between Helen and him— he had walked me home to my apartment. I asked him up for tea. To my surprise, he accepted. We had tea—and then he spent the night. I'm not ashamed of what I did. Nor am I sorry that I did it either." She said the last a bit defiantly, though I thought I could see a tear in her eye.

"As I said, Florence, I try not to judge people if I can help it. I've heard a lot of bad things from a lot of bad people. What you've just told me isn't one of them."

She gave me that crooked little smile again, despite the tear.

"That wasn't the last time, of course. Though it wasn't mostly about the sex. We'd have dinner together when Charles could arrange it. Very discretely, of course. Mostly here, or at some restaurant in Chinatown where we were unlikely to run into anyone that knew Charles. Usually, we'd just talk. I think Charles had become a very lonely man despite his marriage. He just wanted moments of companionship."

That seemed to be the end of the story, at least as far as Florence was concerned.

"You know that you didn't have to tell me any of this?"

"Oh, I think I did, James. I think I wanted to."

"There is one question that I have to ask. As a detective, you understand."

"What's that, James?"

"When was the last time that you had dinner with Charles Mauston?"

"Yes, I can see why you'd have to ask that. As a detective. The answer is, the night he was killed. We had dinner here."

"What time did you leave?"

"I'm not sure. I think about nine. You can ask Mr. Tran." She indicated the waiter. "He might remember."

"And did you go back to your apartment?"

"I did. Charles went back to his office. He said he had some work to do."

"Did he mention whether he was expecting to meet anyone?"

"No. I think he was just going to take care of some paperwork. He did that often. I think he was using it as an excuse not to go home."

"And his mood wasn't out of the ordinary? He didn't seem agitated or as if something was on his mind?"

"No, nothing like that. We had a quiet dinner. He had Mr. Tran call a cab for me. I gave him a kiss on the cheek and then went home. That was the last time I saw him alive." I could see that the thought was hard for her.

"Look, Florence. I'll be honest with you. You probably should have told the police about this. About having dinner with

Mauston, I mean. If they find out on their own it might look suspicious. If they ask me about it, I'll have to tell them what I know. Which is that you had dinner that night. I don't think they need to know anything more."

She nodded.

"There's one more question that I need to ask. Did Mrs. Mauston know about you and her husband? Did she suspect?"

"I'm not sure, James. I don't think so. Frankly, I don't think she would have cared if she had known. It's not as if she still loved Charles. If she ever did. As long as she had money to spend on clothes and things she was satisfied. If she did know, she probably would have been happy that Charles had something to keep him occupied."

"Exactly what do you mean by that?"

"Helen liked to go out, to the theater, nightclubs, dancing, that sort of thing. And she liked to have an escort when she did so. Preferably one that was young and handsome. And had money."

"Someone like Edward Lomax?"

"Yes. Someone like Mr. Lomax—or others."

"There are others?"

"There are, I think, or at least there were. I don't really know the details. It was just gossip, and I really didn't care."

"Was Mr. Mauston aware of this gossip?"

"He never talked about it with me. But I had a feeling that he knew or at least suspected. I think that was one of the things that was making him unhappy. James, you don't think that Helen had anything to do with Charles' murder, do you?"

"I don't know. I do know that she met Lomax that night at the Hotel Alexandria. She left there around ten-thirty, which would have given her plenty of time to get to the office. It was her gun that killed Mauston. I would have thought that it was more likely that she would have talked someone into killing him for her, someone like Lomax, but I think we can rule out Lomax. He wouldn't have had time because he had to catch the night train to Salt Lake City. And I don't buy into the idea of a third conspirator. It would just make things too complex and messy."

"But you think Helen was behind it, don't you?"

"It's as likely as anything right now."

"But why?"

"Did Mauston ever say anything to you about wanting to get a divorce?"

"No."

"Do you think it was a possibility?"

She thought about that for a moment. "Maybe. I know that he wasn't happy."

"That might provide a motive. If there was a divorce, a messy one, where infidelities could be pinned on Mrs. Mauston, she might not end up with much in a divorce settlement, maybe nothing. Compared to that, a quarter of a million in insurance money might not sound half bad. Lomax would end up with the company, which might provide him with a motive if he was involved. I've seen murders committed for a whole lot less, that's for sure."

The reality of it was starting to sink in for her.

"James, what are you going to do?"

"Me? I'm going to do what I always do in these sorts of situations. I'm going to go around asking a lot of awkward questions until someone blinks. Starting with Lomax. I'm still not convinced that he was an active partner in murder, but I want to ask him questions face to face so I can see his reaction."

"James?"

"Yes?"

"Be careful, please."

"That doesn't exactly go with the territory. But my eyes are wide open." The euphoric mood I'd had during dinner had evaporated, replaced by something grimmer. "Let's get out of here."

I offered to take Florence home, but she declined. We compromised by having Mr. Tran call her a taxi. Before she got in, she gave me a kiss. It wasn't on the cheek, either.

15.

I spent the next morning trying to track down Lomax. Calls to all the likely hotels in San Francisco proved negative. If Lomax was staying in one, he wasn't registered under his own name. He wasn't using the name Edgar Larkin anymore, either.

Now, I wasn't really that surprised that I couldn't find Lomax. It's not that hard for a man with a little cash to make himself hard to find if he really wants to. There are plenty of boarding houses and apartments for rent on short terms. As long as you stay away from your usual haunts and overly public places, it can be almost impossible for someone to find you. The real question in my mind was why I couldn't find him. Was he just trying to get away for a few days or was he intentionally lying low because he knew he had become a suspect?

The police might have had better luck running Lomax down, they can put more eyes on the street and have more leverage, but I wasn't quite ready to confide in Lt. Miller. All I really had was a broken alibi, and even that didn't seem to give Lomax enough time to have killed Mauston.

I was running out of leads to follow. There were still a lot of questions swirling around Lomax's fake alibi, but until I could track him down, there didn't seem to be any way for me to resolve them. No one else besides Mrs. Mauston had surfaced as even a plausible suspect.

As I sat there twiddling my mental thumbs, I tried to come up with a reason to involve Florence Bouchet again. Not that I had any reason to suspect her of anything. It just seemed like a good idea. You don't find many women that smart and good looking. It would be a shame to waste the opportunity.

Rummaging around trying to find a match, I usually only smoke when I'm not making progress on a case, I came across the business card that I had pilfered from Mauston's desk.

I took it out and stared at it for a moment. It was a cheap piece of pasteboard, the kind the job printing shops will turn out for a couple of bucks a hundred. It didn't have any logo or artwork, just the name Lance Donovan, the words "Private Detective," and a phone number and address. I had never liked the name Lance, but then I'd never liked Donavan, either. He was the kind of guy who gave the private investigation racket a bad name. He specialized in divorce work, peeking through the keyholes of hotel rooms and that sort of thing. There were rumors that he could be paid to set up compromising situations if the evidence wasn't already there, but so far he'd managed to keep his license.

He'd been a cop down in Daly City until he had gotten caught on the take. Donavan insisted that he had been set up. That was possible, but considering the reputation of the Daly City P.D., he would have had to really have pissed off someone for that to have happened. Again, knowing Donavan, that was certainly a possibility. He had that kind of personality.

I didn't like him, and he didn't like me, but the realities of doing business in a city like San Francisco meant that we maintained a state of armed neutrality towards each other. I decided to give him a call.

"Donavan Investigations." It was Donavan himself. He couldn't afford a receptionist, either. He had a voice that reminded you of the kind of guy who sells brushes door to door, the kind that you wouldn't let off the front stoop into your house.

"Donavan, this is Jim Tolliver."

"Tolliver. Good to hear from you." He wasn't fooling either of us, but at least the conversation was starting out civil.

"Yeah, same here. It's been a while."

"What can I do for you, Jimmy?" He knew that I didn't like being called Jimmy by people that I didn't like.

"I'm just looking for some information in relation to a case I'm working on, Lance. I thought you might be able to help me out."

"What's the case?"

"I'm looking into the death of Charles Mauston."

"I thought that the cops had decided that it was a suicide—"

"Yeah, at least that's the story they're feeding to the newspapers. Maybe it was a suicide, but I've been hired by the widow to prove that it wasn't. It's a matter of her collecting the insurance."

"Insurance, eh." The mention of money always got Donavan's attention.

"Yeah. There's a clause in the policy so that it doesn't pay out for suicide." I didn't mention how much the policy was for. If I had, Donovan would have started to figure out a way to work around me to get a share.

"Well, you know I've got my client's confidentiality to protect—"

"I don't think that will be a problem."

"We'll see, but go ahead and shoot. What do you want to know?"

"It's just this, while I was checking out Mauston's desk I came across one of your business cards. I was wondering if you had done some business for him."

"Well, I don't know, Jimmy. That's kind of privileged information. I don't know that it would be ethical for me to comment on it."

"I have a feeling that Mauston isn't in a position to complain."

Donovan thought that was funny. "Yeah, I guess not. Sure, I did some work for Mauston."

"Do you mind telling me the nature of that work?"

"I don't know, Jimmy—"

"It won't go any further, Lance. Consider it a matter of professional courtesy. One shamus to another."

"You always did have a way with words, Jimmy."

"Well, how about it?"

"I guess it will be alright. But you owe me one. Mauston wanted me to follow his wife. Seems he thought she might be messing around."

"Well, was she?"

"Not that I could prove. I tailed her for a week and got nothing definite. She ran into a couple of guys that she seemed to know in some nightclub. They had a few drinks, danced a dance or two, but nothing more. If she was having an affair, she was being very clever or very discrete about it."

"I see. Did Mauston seem upset about it?"

"Not that I could see. He thanked me when I gave him my report and paid me off. That was the last I heard from him. Either he dropped it, or he went with someone else."

"The guys she met, did any of them have names?"

"I'm sure they did, Jimmy," Donavan replied trying to sound clever.

"Anybody, I might know?"

"Well, one was Mauston's partner. Lomax, I think his name is. But that really just seemed to be a chance meeting, I swear to God. Lomax was at a club with another guy like maybe for business. Mrs. Mauston came in with another woman, seemed to recognize Lomax and went over to say hello. Lomax asked them to join them. They did. They had a round of drinks, danced for a bit, had a late supper there at the club, and then the two women went home. Lomax and his friend hung around for another hour. It was all pretty innocent if you ask me."

"How'd Mauston react when you told him about it."

"He didn't seem to care much one way or the other. I got the impression he had been trolling the waters to see if he had any grounds for divorce, but that was just my impression. Like I said, I made my report, and that was the end of it as far as I was concerned. Was that what you wanted to know?"

"Pretty much. Thanks for the info."

"Funny thing, though—"

"What's that?"

"Shortly after that Mrs. Mauston hired me to check up on her husband."

"Wasn't that a little unethical?" I jibed.

"Nah. I wasn't working for Mr. Mauston anymore by that time, so it was okay." Like I said, Donovan has a pretty flexible sense of morality.

"Did you find anything?" I wasn't sure I wanted to know the answer, but I had to ask the question anyway.

"Yeah, that's the funny part. It turns out that old man Mauston was keeping this Chinese half-breed girl on the side, the one that works in his shop. Mostly they'd just meet for dinner someplace in Chinatown, but sometimes they'd go back to the girl's apartment."

My blood ran cold for a moment. I'd been hoping to keep Florence out of this mess if I could, but now it was starting to look like that might not be possible.

"What did Mrs. Mauston say when you told her about it?"

"That's the odd part, Jimmy. It was almost as if she was glad her husband was having an affair. She just got this odd little smile on her face. I don't know, maybe she liked the idea of having something to hold over her husband's head."

"You haven't told anyone else about this, have you? Like Lt. Miller?"

"Nope. Nobody's asked. And the police and I don't exactly get along these days."

"I'd appreciate it if you kept it that way, Donavan."

"Sure thing. But remember, Jimmy, you owe me one now."

"I'll keep that in mind."

The call had given me something to think about. Donavan had been right about one thing; it had looked like Mauston had been contemplating divorce. You don't hire a detective to tail your wife just on a whim. Financially, a divorce would have been a disaster for Mrs. Mauston if her husband had been able to prove infidelity on her part. It would probably have meant little or no settlement or alimony.

But, had Mauston really been serious about a divorce or had he just been suspicious of his wife? Had he dropped the idea when Donovan's report came back negative? Had he been motivated by jealousy, or had he become infatuated with Florence Bouchet and wanted to divorce his wife so that he would be free to marry the younger woman? There was probably no way to know the answers to these questions now that he was dead.

Perhaps more importantly, at least in regards to his murder, had Mrs. Mauston known about his suspicions? Had she known that she was being followed around? Had she known that Mauston was contemplating divorce? Had she hired Donovan so as to have something to counter any claims of infidelity on

Mauston's part? And, did knowing about the affair make it more or *less* likely that she had a motive for murder?

Was I doing what I had been hired to do? Did that matter? It was looking to me more and more like Mauston *had* been murdered, but the evidence wasn't necessarily pointing in a direction I liked. And how much of what I had found out was I going to tell my client?

A little after noon, I got a phone call from Mrs. Mauston.

"I haven't heard from you for several days, Mr. Tolliver. Have you been avoiding me." She was using that voice that women who are on the edge of middle age sometimes use when talking to men. Earlier I might have found it amusing; now it was just irksome.

"No, ma'am. I've been busy working. It's what you've been paying me to do, remember?"

"Oh, I remember. As long as we're on the subject, have you found anything out, anything that would be helpful."

"There have been, let's say, some developments."

"You're teasing me, Mr. Tolliver. What kind of developments?"

"It's complex. I'm not sure that I can explain it all over the phone."

"Then perhaps we should meet."

"I think that would be for the best."

"This evening, then. My place, shall we say around sevenish?"

"That works for me."

"I'll be waiting with anticipation, then, Mr. Tolliver. Until this evening."

The line went dead. I sat there a moment with the receiver in my hand. Then I set it back in its cradle. I had a feeling that it was going to be an interesting evening.

16.

I was met at the door by the maid. She went through the ritual of taking my hat and depositing it on the hall table before ushering me into the living room.

Mrs. Mauston was waiting for me. She was dressed in a red gown that covered her while leaving little to the imagination. It was the sort of dress women wear in the movies when they want to seduce a man. I wondered who it was intended for.

"Mr. Tolliver, how good of you to come. That will be all for the moment, Ada." The maid withdrew, leaving us alone.

"Can I offer you a cocktail? Or is a whiskey and soda more your style?"

"Either one works for me," I answered.

She spent a few moments at a tray on the sideboard. She seemed to know her way around a cocktail shaker, and I can't say that it was unpleasant watching her at work. She poured the results into a martini glass and added an olive. Ice cubes, whiskey, and a splash of soda went into a tumbler. The latter she handed to me then took the martini glass for herself, holding it delicately by the stem.

"Cheers, Mr. Tolliver."

"Cheers, Mrs. Mauston," I responded.

"There's no need to be so formal, Mr. Tolliver. Why don't you call me Helen?"

"In that case, my given name is Jim."

"Is that what people call you? Jim?" she asked coyly.

"Those that are my friends," I responded.

"And do you consider me to be one of your friends?"

It was obvious that she was playing a game. I saw no reason not to participate.

"Close enough."

She looked at me enigmatically, as if trying to judge what I had meant by the last remark.

"You said that there had been developments, Jim."

"Yes. A number of them, mostly having to do with Edward Lomax's alibi."

"But I thought that the police had verified that he was in Salt Lake City." She seemed to have conveniently forgotten that she was the one who had tipped me off to the Alexandria.

"Oh, he was. At least part of the time. The problem is that part of the time that he said he was in Salt Lake City he was also here in San Francisco staying at the Hotel Alexandria under the name Edgar Larkin. I've got two solid witnesses that can place him there the night your husband was killed as well as another witness who saw him aboard the overnight train back to Salt Lake City."

"I see—" She took a sip of her martini. "You can't think that Edward had anything to do with Charles's murder, do you, Jim?"

"I not sure what to think, Helen. The fact is, is that Lomax lied about where he was that night. That doesn't look good. Not to me, and it won't look good to the police, either."

"Then you haven't told them yet?" I couldn't tell whether it was alarm or excitement that lent an edge to her question.

"No, not yet. I've been trying to get in touch with Lomax to see what he has to say, but he seems to have vanished."

"Why would he do that, Jim, unless he was guilty?"

"Oh, I suspect that he's guilty, alright. I'm just not sure of what."

"I'm not sure that I follow what you're saying, Jim."

I still wasn't sure what the game was that she was playing, but I was sure more than ever that she was playing one. Her reactions were too controlled, too studied, to be natural.

"Lomax was trying to hide the fact that he was in San Francisco that night, but it's not clear that it had anything to do with your husband's death."

"But what other reason could there be, Jim?"

"I have reason to believe that he met a woman at the Hotel Alexandria and that she went up to his room. It's possible that he wanted to keep this rendezvous secret because he was having an affair with this woman and that this woman was married."

I was watching her eyes as I said that, her green eyes the color of old ice. They froze for a moment, motionless, before she blinked. There was no other expression on her face, not even curiosity.

"Have you identified the woman?"

"No. Unfortunately, it seems that she was facing away from the only witness."

"That's too bad. She might have been able to corroborate Edward's story."

"Yes, it is too bad. Just out of curiosity, where were you that night, Helen?"

Again, there was the frozen moment before she responded.

"Me? Why I was here. I've told the police that. Ada confirmed it. You can ask her yourself if you like."

As if on cue, the maid appeared.

"I don't think that will be necessary, Helen."

"Dinner is ready, Mrs. Mauston," Ada announced.

"Thank you, Ada. I took the liberty of having Ada prepare a light supper if that's alright with you, Jim."

"Oh, it's fine by me, Helen. I never refuse free food."

"I was hoping that would be your answer," sounding more like a school girl than a widow.

We went into the dining room. The table had been set for two. I noticed that there was a bottle of champagne in a bucket of ice. I wondered if this was for my benefit or whether Mrs. Mauston always ate like this. Or was it both? Ada poured a glass for each of us and then withdrew.

The dinner proceeded in silence broken only by the clink of silverware and comments related to the food.

Finally, at the end of the meal Mrs. Mauston began:

"I find myself in a delicate position, Jim. I am in need of friends, and I find I have none."

I said, "I'm not sure what you mean," though I was getting a pretty good idea.

"I'll speak bluntly. I need that insurance money. I can't continue to live like this without it. Oh, I shall be able to survive, but I want to do more than that, Jim. You can understand that, can't you?" Her voice was rising, though not yet shrill.

"Oh, I can understand your wanting the money. Most people would."

"But it's more than that, Jim. A woman, a woman like me, needs someone to look after her. Before he died, I had Charles, but now—"

"Don't you have friends, family?"

"None to speak of. I thought at first that I could rely on Edward—as Charles's partner—but with what you've told me tonight, I can see that I can't count on his support. It's clear that he must have been the one responsible for my husband's death."

"I said his alibi was a bust; I didn't say that he killed your husband. I've no proof of that." Earlier I hadn't gone into the fact that Lomax likely hadn't had time to commit the murder. I decided I would keep that to myself for the moment.

"No, that's right, you didn't. But, in a way, though, it might be better for me if he had killed Charles. That is if you *could* prove it." Her voice was taking on a note of—not hysterics, but excitement.

"I'm not sure I'm getting the drift of what you're saying, Helen."

"You must think me a terrible person, Jim." She had moved closer to me as she talked. Now she took my hand in hers.

"It's not that—" I protested.

"It's just that I need someone I can count on now. Someone that can help ensure that I get what is coming to me."

"Don't get me wrong, Helen. If Lomax killed your husband, I'll prove it—"

"Is there any doubt?" She wasn't a woman verging on hysterics anymore. She suddenly sounded cold and logical. "After all, he lied about his alibi. He lied to the police. That makes him the most likely suspect, doesn't it? And he stood to gain ownership of the firm. Who else would have had a motive?"

"What you're saying is all true, but—"

"That's all I'm asking, Jim. You have the evidence that Edward lied. You can turn that over to the police; you *must* turn it over to the police, it's your duty. But you can also help them along in the way they interpret that evidence, a way that will lead them to conclude that Edward is guilty."

"But *is* he guilty?"

"Does it matter? Someone is guilty. Why *can't* it be Edward?" I didn't know if that leap of logic was the way her mind worked—or the way she wanted it to work.

"I'm not sure that's the way things work, Helen."

She turned away from me for a moment. When she turned back, those cold green eyes were fixed on mine.

"I don't suppose you are a wealthy man, Jim."

"I probably wouldn't be a private detective if I were." It wasn't a joke.

"Just think for a moment what you could do with that insurance money, Jim."

"But I wouldn't be getting that money, Helen. That money would be yours."

"Jim, I've been telling you all along that I need someone to look after me, a man to look after me. You could be that man. And if you were, that money would be yours as well as mine."

She had stepped very close to me as she made this speech. She reached up and pressed her lips against mine. I found my hands clasping her around the waist as if they were out of my control, pulling her tight against me.

We stood like that in an embrace for a minute or more before I pushed back. As I did so, I caught sight of her eyes again, those cold, calculating eyes of green ice.

"It's a tempting offer, Helen. If we could pull it off. But it's going to take more than what I've got on Lomax to convince Miller. For a cop, he's not so dumb."

"But you can convince the lieutenant, Jim. One way or another."

I was getting a clearer idea of what that meant, at least in her mind.

"If Lomax is guilty, I'll pin it on him."

"I'm sure you will, Jim. I have every confidence in you."

She moved away from me. She poured what was left of the champagne into a glass and drank.

"Think about it, Jim. Think about the money—and me. Would it be so wrong? After all, Edward may actually be guilty."

I wasn't sure how to respond to that. It was clear that, at least in Helen's mind, the question of Lomax's actual guilt was irrelevant. It was clear, as well, that I was being offered— something—if I arranged for the police to charge Lomax with her husband's murder. It made me wonder what, if anything, she had offered Lomax.

"If you'll excuse me for a moment, I want to tell Ada that she can clear up and go to bed. Why don't you wait for me in the living room? Fix yourself a drink if you like."

She disappeared towards the kitchen. I went back to the living room and poured a stiff glass of Scotch. I didn't bother with soda or ice.

I stood at the window, looking out at the bay over the tops of the buildings across the street. Maybe the champagne and whiskey were going to my head. Was I being a fool? Two hundred and fifty thousand dollars was a lot of money, even if shared, more than I was ever likely to come by honestly. I didn't know that Lomax wasn't guilty, not for sure. But I had my suspicions.

"It's a beautiful view, isn't it, Jim," Helen said. Her voice was almost wistful, the hardness gone.

"Yeah, that's one of the reasons I've stuck around. You don't get views like this where I came from."

"Where did you come from, Jim?"

"Here, there," I equivocated. I didn't feel like revealing any more about myself than I had to. "Sometimes I'm not sure anymore."

She seemed to sense my change in mood for she said, "It's getting late."

I glanced at the clock on the wall. It was after one. I tossed off the last of the Scotch.

"I guess I'd better get going then."

"Perhaps that would be best, Jim. But think about what I said, won't you?"

"You can count on it, Helen. Good-night. I'll see myself out."

I picked up my hat from the table next to the door. There was no sign of the maid. I thought she must have gone to bed already. After all, it was late.

I rode the automatic elevator down to the empty lobby. The doorman wasn't on duty at that hour.

Outside on the sidewalk, I felt a cold, damp wind coming off the bay. I pulled the lapels of my coat up around my neck. There wasn't a cab in sight, so I started to hoof it towards Market where I hoped I might have better luck.

I'd gone maybe halfway to the corner when I felt the hairs on the back of my neck stiffen. I looked back, but there was no one there. Too much whiskey and not enough sleep. I took a few more steps and thought I had heard something. I started to turn, but I never completed the motion.

A bright light exploded in my head, and then everything went black. The last thing that I remembered was that it hadn't been a man.

17.

The next few hours were a blur as I slid in and out of consciousness. The first thing that I was aware of clearly was of a white-clad nurse holding my wrist while she took my pulse. She wrote something down on the chart at the end of my bed, then looked up and saw that my eyes were open.

"So we're awake now, are we, Mr. Tolliver?" She had the bedside manner of a spinster fourth-grade teacher and a face to match, which was just as well. I wasn't feeling up to a hospital romance.

"What happened?" Not the brightest remark, but at least it was pertinent.

"Someone tried to beat your brains out. That is unless you slipped and fell. There was alcohol on your breath when they brought you in." I could sense the disapproval in her voice as if I had spelled a word wrong.

"Do they know who hit me?"

"If they do, they didn't tell me. If it's not on your chart, it's none of my business. You just take it easy, Mr. Tolliver. You've taken a hard knock. The doctor thinks you may have a concussion."

That seemed like good advice. I lay back and stared at the paint on the ceiling.

A couple of hours later, or maybe fifteen minutes, the nurse was back. She took my pulse again and seemed to approve of the results.

"There's a policeman to see you. A lieutenant. Do you feel up to it? If not, I can chase him away."

"No, might as well let him in. If you don't, he'll just come back again."

She went out into the hall and returned a moment later with Lt. Miller.

"You can only stay for fifteen minutes, Lieutenant. And don't tire him out."

"I'll go easy on the third degree, nurse."

The nurse looked at Miller suspiciously, not sure if he was joking, but left the room.

"So what have you gotten yourself into, Jimmy?"

"You tell me. I was on my way home when the lights went out."

"Did you see who did it?"

"Not really. I got this sense of someone coming up behind me, but before I had a chance to turn I got hit. After that, I don't remember anything until I woke up here a few hours ago."

I didn't add that I had this half-remembered impression that the person behind me had been a woman. It was all very vague and dreamlike. For all I knew, it was a memory of a nurse from some moment of lucidity once they had brought me to the hospital. The nurse and the woman in my dreams had had much the same build.

"Yeah. The doc said that with a head injury like yours even if you had seen anything you might not remember it. As it is, it's lucky for you a beat cop came around the corner just as you went down. Otherwise—well, we wouldn't be having this conversation."

"Did the cop see anything?"

"Not good enough to tell who it was. Just someone, maybe a little over medium height, wearing an overcoat and a hat pulled down low."

I grunted. As a description, it was pretty much worthless.

"Robbery?"

"If it was, they didn't get anything. You still had your wallet and gun on you. What's with the gun, Jimmy? You don't usually pack one unless you're expecting trouble."

"Well I found it, didn't I?"

"Yeah, sure," Miller replied. He was looking more like a cop and less like a friend. "So what aren't you telling me?"

"What makes you think I've got anything to tell?"

"Because someone seems to have wanted to keep you from telling it. Permanently. So what were you doing at the Mauston dame's place?"

"In case you don't remember, she's my client. I was making a report."

"At one o'clock at night?" Miller asked suspiciously. "An odd time to be visiting a lady. Some people might think the two of you were up to something."

"It was strictly business, Miller."

"Sure it was, Jimmy. But I'm Homicide, not Vice, so I'm guessing this is about her husband. She hired you to prove that it was murder, not suicide. So maybe you got conked on the noggin because you've succeeded, or at least were coming too close for comfort for someone."

"I haven't proved anything, lieutenant."

"No, but I think you've got some suspicions. So what gives, Tolliver? Withholding evidence is a crime in this state."

"I'm not withholding anything, Miller. Nothing that I can prove."

Miller looked me in the eye. It hurt. Everything hurt. All I wanted was for Miller to disappear so I could go back to feeling sorry for myself.

"I did find out one thing," I said slyly.

"What's that, Jimmy?"

"It's about Lomax. He wasn't in Salt Lake City that night like he said. He was right here in San Francisco."

Miller shook his head. "We checked his alibi, Jimmy. He was checked into a hotel in Salt Lake that night. He was on the night train from there that didn't arrive in San Francisco until the next day. The attendant on the sleeping car confirmed that."

"Yeah. That's because he was. But he was also checked into the Hotel Alexandria the night Mauston was killed. Except he wasn't registered as Edward Lomax. He used the name Edgar Larkin. He probably took a woman up to his room. I haven't been able to identify the woman. Later, he had dinner alone at the restaurant in the hotel around eleven. Then he caught the midnight train to Salt Lake City."

"How'd you find all this out, Jimmy?"

"I played detective and asked. You should try it sometime, lieutenant."

"Who'd you ask?"

"The house dick, the night clerk, and the maitre d' at the hotel restaurant. Oh, and I talked to the sleeping car attendant on the train, too, the one that vouched for Lomax being on the train the next day. It turns out that the night before he was working the midnight train from San Francisco to Salt Lake. He said he saw Lomax drinking in the club car. That's why he thought it was odd that he was on the train back from Salt Lake the next night."

"He didn't say anything about that to me," Miller said with annoyance.

"Did you ask him?"

"Well—" Miller paused then continued sheepishly, "no, I didn't ask him."

"That's your problem, Miller. That and the fact that maybe I slipped the attendant a couple of bucks for his cooperation."

"The taxpayers don't give us any money for bribes, Jimmy," Miller said shaking his head again. "Why should I believe this story? Maybe the attendant made it up just to string you along and earn himself a few dollars."

"I believe him, Miller. He didn't have any reason to lie. I'd already given him cash when he told me about Lomax. Besides, I checked the passenger list for the train to Salt Lake. There wasn't any Lomax on the list—but there *was* an Edgar Larkin."

"So you think Lomax killed Mauston? Why didn't you tell me all this when you found it out?"

"Because I don't think Lomax did it, that's why. The times don't work out. He was having dinner at the Alexandria at ten-thirty. He caught the train to Salt Lake City at a little after midnight. Given that there's a thirty-minute ferry ride in between, that doesn't leave him much time to get to Mauston's office and shoot him, does it? Not the way I figure it, anyhow."

"Then why did he lie about being in San Francisco that night, and why did he give us a phony alibi?"

"Yeah. Why? That's what I'd like to ask him. Except I haven't been able to find him. I spent most of yesterday trying to run him to ground with no luck."

"Well, I can take care of that. I'll put out an A.P.B. for his arrest as a material witness."

"You do that, lieutenant. Look, maybe I should have told you this sooner, but, like I said, I don't think Lomax did it. At least I don't think he was the guy that pulled the trigger."

"Still, you should have told me," Miller said, sounding like a cop again. "I'll let it slide this time, Jimmy. Just this once."

"That's mighty white of you, Miller. But getting back to more personal matters, what are you going to do about my getting hit over the head?"

"What do you expect me to do, Jimmy. We got no description that's worth a hill of beans. I'm already looking for this Lomax guy. Who else is out there gunning for you, Jimmy?"

"Damned if I know. There's been some guy that's been tailing me. He claimed he worked for the insurance company. Said his name was Mandelbrot."

"Mandelbrot is legit, Jimmy. He does work for the insurance company. Besides, why would he want to kill you?"

"I don't know. Maybe he gets a cut of the quarter of a million if the insurance company doesn't have to pay out on Mauston. Maybe it's a part of his incentive plan."

"I think that conk on the noggin has scrambled your brains, Jimmy."

"Okay, it probably wasn't Mandelbrot that sandbagged me. The fact remains that someone tried to take me out, probably because I'm getting too close."

"Who, Jimmy? Give me a name."

"I wish I could, Miller, believe me, I wish I could."

I was about to say more when the nurse came in and shooed Miller out.

After he left, I tried to rest, but that last question kept running through my brain. Who did want me out of the way? It might have been Lomax, but only if he really had been part of a conspiracy to kill Mauston. But I couldn't make the pieces of the puzzle fit around him. If he had hired someone to do in Mauston, then why hadn't he just stayed put in Salt Lake establishing an alibi that couldn't be broken? Why had he been in San Francisco that night at all? It didn't make sense.

I'd thrown Mandelbrot's name out to Miller mostly just to have something to say. Insurance companies aren't necessarily the most ethical entities, but they didn't normally go around knocking off inconvenient people. Of course, maybe Mandelbrot had been acting on his own. Maybe he *would* be paid a percentage of what the company didn't have to pay out. It was a stretch, but not impossible.

So who did that leave? Some Chinese gang? The Russians? That seemed even more unlikely. Our parting at the tea room hadn't been exactly amicable, but that still didn't give them a reason to try and bash my brains in.

It kept coming back to the same person, Mrs. Mauston. She had as much as admitted to having an affair with Lomax. She'd known that Lomax had been in town that night. I didn't buy the fact that a friend of hers had just happened to see Lomax at the Alexandria. She had fed me that information to blow his alibi, hoping that would pin the murder on Lomax.

Maybe Mauston *had* been planning to divorce her. If so, there was a good chance that she wouldn't have come out so well. Mauston might have been able to prove infidelity on her part. In those circumstances, two hundred and fifty grand might have seemed like it was worth the risk.

But could she have done it? She had had the opportunity. If she had been the woman Lomax had met at the Alexandria, she had left the hotel in plenty of time to get to Far Eastern for the murder. Even if she hadn't had a key, Mauston would likely have let her in without thinking about it. And it *had* been her gun that he'd been killed with.

I'm not one of those idealists who put women on a pedestal and think they can do no wrong. I've known women that were murderers. Was Helen Mauston one of them? Could she have killed her husband in cold blood? Because if she *had* killed him, it would have been as part of a complex plan and not some spur of the moment crime of passion. Did I think she could do it? Did I want to?

And if she had killed him, why had she hired a private investigator to prove that it was murder? Was that part of the plan? Where did that put me?

They kept me in the hospital overnight for "observation." I spent the time going over and over the same arguments, but I couldn't come up with any good conclusions.

In the morning they fed me a breakfast of cold scrambled eggs and weak coffee. I still had a bandage wrapped around my head to hold it together. After breakfast, I had to fill out a stack of forms, most of which said that anything that happened to me wasn't the hospital's fault. It was nearly noon before I walked out of there a free man.

18.

I should have gone home and gone to bed. I didn't. I wanted to find Lomax. I wasn't sure that he was the one that had clocked me from behind. At that point, I wasn't sure of anything, but I had an idea that one way or another, Lomax was the key. All I had to do was find him.

He'd been dodging me the last few days, or at least that's what I thought he'd been doing. Making phone calls wasn't working. Maybe what was needed was the personal touch. Somebody at his office must have some idea where he was.

I grabbed a taxi outside the hospital and gave the driver Far Eastern's address. I was in no shape to ride a cable car, and I was still working on Mrs. Mauston's dime anyway. When the cabbie dropped me off, he asked if I wanted him to wait. Maybe it was the bandage sticking out from under my hat that made him ask. I said no, but gave him an extra quarter tip for asking.

I was about to ring the bell for the office when I got a better idea and entered the shop instead. Florence looked up from behind the counter when she heard the sound of the door. I caught a smile crossing her beautiful face for a moment when she saw who it was, but it quickly turned to a frown. I was hoping that that was because of the state of my noggin.

"James! What happened?" The concern in her voice almost made up for my getting slugged from behind. Almost.

"This? It's nothing. Somebody cold-cocked me from behind."

"It doesn't look like nothing, James. Are you all right?" She reached out, and I felt the tips of her fingers on the side of my face. That did more for my head than the pills the doctor had given me.

"The doc said I'll be alright in a few days. I feel OK except for the headache."

She looked at me dubiously. "I thought you private detectives could take care of yourselves."

"Yeah. Well, like I said, it was dark and whoever hit me came at me from behind. I didn't have a chance to get a good lick in."

"You should be more careful, James." She sounded like she wanted to mother me. I could think of worse things. Lots of worse things.

"I guess I picked the wrong line of work for that," I said trying to joke it off.

Florence didn't think it was funny. "When did this happen?"

"The night before last. I was leaving Mrs. Mauston's—"

I caught the look of disapproval on her face. I wasn't sure if it was jealousy—or something else.

"You don't think much of Mrs. Mauston, do you?" I asked.

"No, not particularly. Maybe it's because I see her for the gold-digger that she is behind that polished exterior of hers." She said it with that particular venom that women reserve for each other.

"Say, you aren't jealous, are you?" I teased.

She didn't need to say anything. I could tell what she felt from the blush that came to her oriental cheekbones. It was quite attractive.

"You can relax. It was all business. I just stopped by to make a report on my progress in solving her husband's murder."

"Have you made any?" I could tell there was more than curiosity behind the question.

"Some. Enough that it appears someone wants to stop me."

She paused a moment while the implication of that sank in. "You should be careful, James. I wouldn't want anything to happen to you."

"Trust me, neither do I."

"Why are you here, James? Shouldn't you be resting?"

"That's what the doc said, but what does he know. But you're right; I did come for something other than your sympathy. I'm looking for your boss, Lomax. I've been trying to get in touch with him for a couple of days, but I haven't been having much luck. I thought that I'd check the situation out in person."

"You don't think that he had anything to do with Charles' death, do you?"

"I don't know. I do know that he's been behaving pretty suspiciously for an innocent man. That just might be because he's running scared, but I think he knows more about what happened than he told the cops. That's why I need to sit down and have a long talk with him."

"I wish I could help you, James, but I'm afraid I can't. I haven't seen Mr. Lomax now for several days."

"What about upstairs?" I gave a nod to the offices above us. It made my head hurt.

"Not that I know of, but then I don't go up there often."

"You don't mind if I take the back way up and see for myself, do you?"

She smiled at that. I decided that I liked her smile.

"I don't see why not. You know the way."

"Thanks." I headed toward the door into the back.

"James—"

"Yes?"

"Please be careful." She said it in that exasperated tone mothers use with their little boys knowing it won't have much effect. I just waved and let the door shut behind me.

Going up the back way would let me catch the office off guard. I didn't necessarily think that anyone was trying to hide things from me, but I didn't want to give them the opportunity, either.

Climbing the stairs from the warehouse proved to be more of a chore than I had planned on. I paused a moment at the top to catch my breath before opening the door into the office.

The Chinese typist gave me a smile as I walked in.

"Say, doll, Mr. Lomax wouldn't happen to be in, would he?"

"No, Mr. Tolliver, he hasn't been in for several days," she replied. As an afterthought, she added, "Would you like to speak to Mr. Nilgren?"

"I'd much rather chat with you, but I suppose I'd better talk to the man in charge."

I didn't have much choice in the matter. Nilgren came out of Lomax's office. He didn't look particularly pleased to see me.

"Mr. Tolliver," he acknowledged. "Is there anything I can do for you?"

"Yeah. I'd like to speak to Mr. Lomax."

"Quite frankly, so would I. As I told you on the phone, he hasn't been into the office in several days. It's made things quite difficult. There are decisions that have to be made and with him gone and Mr. Mauston—"

"With Mr. Mauston dead," I completed his sentence. "Yes, I can see where that might cause you problems. I've got a few matters to discuss with him myself."

"Yes. Well, as I explained he isn't here."

"And you don't know where he can be reached?"

"Have you tried his apartment?"

"Have you?"

"Yes. The building super says that he hasn't seen Mr. Lomax for several days. He was under the impression that he was out of town. His car hasn't been at the garage where he keeps it, either." His implication was that if I was a detective, I should have checked those places. I had.

"So you don't know where he is?"

"No. I've told you that Mr. Tolliver." I could sense that Nilgren was getting a little short tempered on the subject, which was fine by me. Maybe he'd forget himself and make a slip.

"You wouldn't happen to know of someplace he might go if he wanted to get away, would you?"

"Mr. Lomax never discussed matters of his personal life with me."

I could see I wasn't going to get anywhere trying to pump Nilgren. Either he really didn't know, or he wasn't going to tell me.

"I noticed that you came out of Lomax's office just now."

"Yes. I needed to get some papers. Some of us still have work to do around here."

"You wouldn't mind if I took a look for myself, would you?"

"I assure you, Mr. Tolliver, that Mr. Lomax isn't in there hiding, but if you want to see for yourself, I suppose I can't stop you."

I took that for a yes. At least I didn't wait for him to try and prevent me. He had been right, though. Lomax wasn't in his office, and there wasn't a back door which he could have used to give me the slip.

I took the opportunity to give Lomax's desk the once over. I needn't have bothered. There was nothing that gave a clue as to where Lomax might have gotten himself to. I leafed through his desk calendar, but that was mostly blank. I even checked the pad of paper next to the telephone. I know that in mystery novels the detective usually finds an important clue by using a pencil to reveal an impression of what had been written on a sheet that had been torn off. Lomax must not have read any of those books, because he hadn't bothered to leave a forwarding address for me to find.

There wasn't much point in my hanging around. If Lomax hadn't shown up in the last few days, the chances were that he wasn't going to walk in the door in the next few minutes. I told Nilgren that I'd let myself out and left using the front stairs.

I should have gone home then and gone to bed. Instead, I went back to the office. When I checked with the telephone girl and asked if there were any messages, she said no, but that the same man had kept calling. He hadn't left a message, but he had left his name. It was Edward Lomax.

19.

I hung around the office for a couple of hours waiting for the phone to ring. It finally did. It was Lomax.

"Tolliver, is that you?" It sounded like he'd been drinking. He wasn't drunk yet, but he was getting there.

"It was, the last time I looked."

"We've got to talk."

"That's fine by me. I've been looking for you the last couple of days to do just that."

"You have?" Lomax seemed surprised.

"Yeah. I've got a few questions about your alibi I'd like to ask. Where are you?"

"I'm somewhere out of town."

"I figured as much. You know the police are looking for you, too, don't you?"

"They are?"

"Yeah, I think they've got some questions of their own they'd like to ask."

This seemed to be news to Lomax. There was silence for a moment, but the line wasn't dead.

"Say, Lomax. You weren't in San Francisco two nights ago, were you?"

"No. Why do you ask?" He sounded puzzled about the question, as if he didn't know that that was when I'd gotten conked on the head. Maybe he didn't.

"Just curiosity."

"Like I said, I'm out of town. I've been out of town for a few days." Either he hadn't been the one who had slugged me, or he was a great actor.

"So where are you?"

"Look, Tolliver, I need your help. I'm in big trouble, and I want to talk to you. You're the only one I trust right now."

I wondered at that. I'd never given him any reason to think I might be on his side. It sounded like something a desperate man might say.

"Okay. But if I'm going to help you, we need to meet."

"Do you promise you'll come alone? No police?"

I wasn't sure what Lomax had in mind, but it looked as if there was only one way to find out.

"You have my word. Alone and no police. Now, where are you?"

"Do you know where Olema is?"

"Vaguely. It's a little burg up the coast, isn't it?"

"Yeah. Just before Point Reyes Station. I'm staying at the hotel there."

"What's the address?"

"Don't worry about the address, Tolliver. You won't have any trouble finding the place."

"When?"

"As soon as you can get here. I'll be waiting for you. I don't have anywhere else to go."

"Okay. It'll take me a few hours."

"It doesn't matter. And Tolliver?"

"Yeah?"

"I didn't kill Charles. You've got to believe me."

"I'll give you a chance to tell me your story, Lomax. That's all I can promise."

The phone line went dead.

Olema is in Marin County, on the north side of the bay. I knew a guy that owned a garage over in Sausalito that rented cars. I gave him a call and asked him to meet me at the ferry landing. After that, I checked my gun and slipped it back into its holster. Gingerly placing my hat on my head, I tried to hide the bandage there as best I could. Then I caught a cab to the Hyde St. Pier.

Gene Corwin was waiting for me at the ferry landing in Sausalito. Gene is one of those guys who is handy with anything mechanical. He thinks he's a businessman, too, and always has a new money-making scheme in the works. He's made a bunch of money, but between booze, gambling, and women he never seems to hang on to it for long. I'd run into him when I first came out to the coast and was still working for Continental. He'd been a big help, and I tried to throw him business whenever I could.

Gene had come to pick me up in a rusting Model A roadster that had had the rear of the body removed and replaced with a truck box for hauling parts. "Gene's Garage" was painted in neat lettering on the doors, but that was about the only thing neat about the truck.

As we drove back to his garage, he kept glancing at me sideways. Finally, his curiosity got the better of him, and he asked, "What happened to you?"

"Somebody sucker punched me from behind." That seemed to be enough explanation for him. He knew the business I was in and the risks involved.

"You okay to drive?"

"I'm okay. It only hurts when I laugh. You got a car for me?"

"Yeah. If you don't mind how it looks, I've got a Buick that's a little dented but runs fine."

"I don't care about how it looks as long as it will get me up the coast and back."

"How far?"

"Olema."

"It'll do that with no problems. It's full of gas, got good tires and a decent spare. I can let you have it for ten bucks for the day if you bring it back in one piece. You *are* planning on bringing it back in one piece, aren't you?" He'd picked up on the fact that I was packing a pistol.

"That's the plan." I had a plan, alright, but I wasn't sure that it matched Lomax's.

"You sure you're okay to drive? I can get someone to drive up with you if you want. I'd offer to go myself, but I've got the business to attend to."

"I'm okay to drive. The person I'm meeting asked that I come alone, so I won't be wanting any help."

Gene looked at me as if calculating the odds that he'd ever see the Buick again.

"Can I still have the car?"

"Sure, Jim. I trust you."

"Look, I'm planning on bringing the car back this evening. If I change my mind, I'll let you know. If I don't come back and you haven't heard from me before closing, give a call to Lt. Miller in Homicide in San Francisco. Tell him I went to Olema. He'll understand."

"It's like that, is it?"

"Yeah, it's like that."

"Okay. Lt. Miller in Homicide."

The car was as he had described it, a two-year-old Buick sedan painted a deep maroon. There was a big dent in the front fender and a scrape along the passenger side door, but when I got in and started the engine, it ran smooth and strong. I handed Gene a sawbuck and was off.

The map I had showed that there were two ways to get to Olema, the coast road and an inland road that ran from San Rafael. I was in no hurry, and it might be good to let Lomax sweat a little. I decided to take the more scenic coast road.

It had been hot in Sausalito, but after I had driven a few miles and was on the coast road, there was a good breeze coming off the ocean that cooled things down nicely. I drove with the windows down. With the sunshine and fresh air, the pounding in my head was starting to subside.

There wasn't much traffic on the road, but it occurred to me that once the bridge over the Golden Gate was finished that there would be a lot more people crossing over to Marin to take in the sights. It probably wouldn't be recognizable in five years, and the road I was on would be clogged with cars every decent weekend. I wondered what that might do to Gene's business, but he'd probably come up with an idea to make money. Maybe he'd open a diner where the tourists could get a sandwich without ever having to leave their cars.

Gene had been right about one thing, the Buick was a good car for the drive, nice and solid. It held the road well, even on the numerous twists and turns of the highway. Mostly the road was flanked by forest, and I could only get glimpses of the ocean, but every once in a while there'd be a break in the trees, and I would get a nice clear view. Very scenic.

I wasn't sure what to expect when I got to Olema. Lomax had sounded like a desperate man, and desperate men do strange things at times. There was a possibility that I was walking into a trap. It must have occurred to him that he was the prime suspect for Mauston's murder. Lomax was the one person that stood to benefit from his death. He and Mrs. Mauston, but she only benefited if it was ruled a murder and not a suicide. That meant someone had to take the rap for the killing. Lomax must have realized that his alibi wouldn't stand up and that it was only a matter of time before the police were after him. That was probably the reason that he was holed up in a place like Olema.

But had he done it? I had my doubts, which was why I hadn't just passed on Lomax's location to Lt. Miller and been done with it. That would have fulfilled my obligation to Mrs. Mauston and kept me out of things. But I could only accept that if I believed that Lomax had done it, and, like I said, I had my doubts. The whole thing didn't quite add up right.

As I was mulling this over, the trees gave way to pasture. It was dairy country, though I knew farmers in the Midwest that would find that hard to believe. I could see the occasional cow chomping on dry, brown grass on the hillsides to my right, as bucolic a scene as you could imagine. Then I reached Olema.

Lomax had been right about my not having any trouble finding the Hotel Olema. Olema was pretty much a one street village, and that street wasn't very long. As I drove in from the south, I passed a sign that read "pop. 55, alt. 66." There was a little building on the right that looked to be part general store and part post office. After that was a road coming in from the east, and just after that, there was a building on the left-hand side of the road that had to be the hotel. There just weren't any other choices.

I parked the car in front of the hotel. It didn't look as though anyone would mind. The place looked like something out of a western movie, a two-story unpainted frame building with a covered porch running the length of the front. There was even a pair of swinging half doors in the entrance. I climbed the steps to the porch and gave the doors a push.

Once inside, it took a moment for my eyes to adjust to the dark. I found myself in a large room. A bar ran along the right side of the room. Lomax was standing at the bar. There was a glass and a half-empty bottle of whiskey on the bar in front of him. He was still wearing the suit that I had last seen him in; only it wasn't neatly pressed anymore. Neither was Lomax. He looked like someone that hadn't slept in a couple of days and who, during that time, had taken most of his nourishment out of the bottle.

He had heard me come in, and when he turned to face me, there was a Colt .45 automatic in his hand. He hadn't been quite fast enough, though. My own pistol was pointing squarely at his chest. It was a face off.

The bartender looked nervously between us, not sure whether he should duck or run. Undecided, he just stood there with a towel in one hand and a glass in the other.

"Are you alone?" Lomax asked.

"I'm alone."

We stood facing each other, guns drawn and aimed at each other for what seemed an eternity but was probably no more than five seconds. Then Lomax gave a little shrug and set his pistol down on the bar.

"Give my friend a beer," he said to the bartender, "that is unless you'd like to join me in some of this gentleman's fine whiskey."

"A beer will do fine. I'm planning on driving back to San Francisco yet this evening."

"A beer it is, then, George."

George, the bartender, still seemed half-paralyzed, but instinct took over. He turned and picked up a beer glass from the back-bar and worked the single tap in the center of the bar.

"It's on me, Tolliver," Lomax said. "I'm running a tab."

I took a swig of the beer when the bartender handed it to me. It was stale and not very cold, but nothing had ever tasted so good. I realized that I was still holding my pistol in the other hand, looking a bit foolish. I put it away.

George seemed to sense that the drama was over and moved to the other end of the bar where he continued to polish a glass. But every few seconds he'd look our direction.

20.

"Have you ever made a fool of yourself over a woman, Tolliver?"

"Once or twice, then I grew up."

He gave me a hurt look, or maybe it was one of contempt. I couldn't be sure.

"I forgot, you're one of those tough guy private eyes, aren't you?" Lomax poured a couple of more fingers of whiskey into his glass. I could almost feel sorry for him. His nice safe world was crashing down around his ears.

"Okay, I deserved that. Yeah, I've met a woman or two that made me do something stupid. I've met more than a few that have made me think about it. But I've never committed murder, not for a woman."

He looked up from his whiskey.

"You've got to believe me, Tolliver. I didn't do it. I didn't kill Charles. No matter what it looks like."

There was a pleading in his eyes, like a puppy that's done something wrong only he doesn't know what it was. I still didn't like the guy, but that I didn't have some sympathy for him.

"I believe you, Lomax. Why don't you tell me what really happened? Or at least your end of it."

"You've met Helen. You know what kind of woman she is."

"Yeah, I've met her."

"She's got all those qualities you dream about in a woman, beauty, charm, wit. She knows how to use those qualities to get her way, too, at least with men."

"Yeah, I've noticed that, too."

"I didn't start out planning to have an affair with her. I admit I like women, and they seem to like me, but Charles was my partner. And maybe I don't have the highest morals, but I'm not stupid. At least I wasn't at first. Far Eastern was a good thing for me. I was making good money doing something that wasn't hard or unpleasant. Why would I want to risk losing that?"

"But then she seduced you. That's what you're saying, isn't it?" I interjected.

"You make it sound so shallow, saying it that way. Like I was some sort of callow schoolboy.   But yes, she seduced me. Sometimes I almost think that she had it all planned out from the beginning, how she arranged for Charles to be murdered and then pin it on me.   Maybe that's giving her too much credit, but beneath that lovely exterior is a cold, calculating machine."

"I've noticed that, too. So she seduced you. When was this?"

"Five, maybe six months ago. I'd known her before that, of course, as my partner's wife. The three of us would have the occasional dinner together, that sort of thing. You'll have to understand, Charles was never a particularly social sort of person. He didn't really like to go out to the theater or things like that. Particularly nightclubs.   He hated nightclubs with a passion. Helen, of course, loved them. The music, the dancing, being seen, especially being seen. The two of them were complete opposites."

"You know, that's something that's puzzled me," I said. "Why did the two of them ever get together in the first place? From what I know of Mauston, he doesn't strike me as being the kind of man that would be attracted to a woman like Helen. He must have had some idea of what he was getting into?"

"It goes back to the fact that all men can make fools of themselves over a woman. I wasn't around at the time, that was before we went into business together, but the way I understand it, they met on a ship returning to the States from Honolulu. Charles had gotten tired of the Orient and was moving back to San Francisco. Helen had gone out to the islands as an actress or a dancer or something like that and had found it just didn't pay. Helen describes their meeting as a 'shipboard romance.' Personally, I think she saw Charles as the richest bachelor on the ship and set her sights on him. At the heart of her, there's a real gold-digger. Charles was looking to settle down. I think he saw the idea of marrying a charming woman as an asset, part of the domestic furniture. Whatever the case may be, the two of them were married shortly after they arrived in California.

"At first I think the marriage was alright. Helen had what she wanted, money, social standing, respectability. Charles, well, he had a beautiful wife to show off. It seemed to have soured pretty quickly, though. They ended up going their separate ways in most things. I don't think either one of them particularly minded."

"So what changed?"

"I'm really not sure, Tolliver. Something did, that's for sure. Charles became less tolerant of Helen's foibles. He spent less time at home and more time working late. Or at least that's what he said. Frankly, I think he just wanted to get away from Helen."

"Did you know he was having an affair?" I asked.

Lomax raised his head, a look of surprise on his face.

"He did? With whom?"

"Miss Bouchet. The woman in the shop?"

"Florence? That old dog. Why he was almost old enough to be her grandfather. That explains a lot, though."

"So you didn't know about Mauston and Florence?"

"No. But then I was out of town a lot."

"Do you think Mrs. Mauston knew about his affair?"

"She never mentioned it to me, if she did. But it's possible. Helen is very clever about things like that."

"Why didn't Mauston just get a divorce?"

"I think he might have been thinking about it towards the end. I know he had several meetings with his lawyers about something. But I think it came down to alimony. I think the idea of Helen getting any of his money irked him so much that he wouldn't go through with it unless he could divorce her for infidelity, and as I said, Helen could be very clever about such things. Also very discrete, in her own way."

"Let's get back to you and Helen," I said, trying to get him to concentrate.

"I'd gotten into the habit of acting as her escort to things that Charles didn't want to bother with, like the theater. All very innocent at first. At least on my part. We'd run into each other at nightclubs, too. Have a drink together, maybe a dance or two.

Just being sociable. Helen can be quite charming company when she puts her mind to it.

"But one night, maybe three months before Charles was killed we ran into each other at a nightclub. I was with a friend, Helen was with a woman that she knows. The woman complained that she had a headache. My friend offered to take her home. That left Helen and me alone together. I'd had maybe a bit too much to drink. I'm not sure about Helen. I can't remember her ever being drunk. Well, one thing led to another, and we ended up in a hotel room."

"I see. Do you think it was planned? On her part, I mean."

"Not at the time, of course. Now I'm not so sure. We started arranging for—trists—whenever I was in town. It was all very torrid and exciting. But then you know what Helen can be like, don't you, Tolliver?"

"It hasn't gotten that far between us, but I understand what you mean. Helen can be very—persuasive. Getting back to business, though. You were seeing each other regularly?"

"At first, but it was getting more difficult for us to meet. Helen suspected that Charles had hired a private detective to shadow her. She insisted that we had to be more discrete."

"How did the night Mauston was murdered come about?"

"As you know, I'd been on an extended business trip out East. I'd been gone for several weeks. While I was in Denver, I received a telegram from Helen saying that she was dying to see me, and couldn't I arrange something so that we could see each other while Charles thought I was out of town. We arranged to meet at the Hotel Alexandria."

"Was that your idea or hers?"

"Hers, I think."

"So what happened that night?"

"I was registered at the hotel in Salt Lake City. I took a train to San Francisco without checking out so that it would look like I was still there. I checked into the Hotel Alexandria. I had booked a seat on the late train to Salt Lake City so that I could check out of the hotel there and come back the next night."

"And Mrs. Mauston met you at the hotel?"

"Yes. She came up to my room. Well, I don't have to explain that to you, do I? But she said that she had to leave early, a little before eleven because Charles had changed his plans and was going to come home. I had a late supper at the restaurant, checked out and just had time to catch the night train back to Salt Lake City. But that proves that I couldn't have killed Charles. Don't you see? The police said that he was killed sometime after midnight. I couldn't have done it and still catch the train. You believe me, don't you?"

"Sure, I believe you. That doesn't mean the cops will. Establishing the time of death is tricky. It's hard to be precise. Why'd you lie about being in San Francisco? That will make the cops suspicious when they find out about it, and they will find out about it." I didn't mention that I'd already told the story to Miller.

"Are you going to tell them?"

"If they ask. But I may not have to tell them anything. No matter what you've heard, they aren't all stupid. The cops may figure it out for themselves given enough time. Somebody may tell them."

"Who? You mean Helen?"

"It's possible. But there's also the hotel dick at the Alexandria. He knows you were there that night. The night clerk may put two and two together, as well. It doesn't matter. The case has become too prominent for things to be kept secret. So why didn't you tell the cops you were at the Alexandria that night?"

"Because Helen asked me not to. She was afraid that if word got out that she had been having an affair, the police might suspect that she had had something to do with Charles's murder. They'd go after her instead of the real killer."

Part of me wanted to slap Lomax on the side of the head. The other part was just too amazed at how dumb a smart guy could be.

"Did you ever think that maybe it all was a bit too convenient?"

"What do you mean?"

"Think about it, Lomax. She just happens to talk you into coming into town the night Mauston is killed, then she talks you into lying to the police about it making you a convenient fall guy if the cops start getting suspicious. Then she hires a two-bit private dick to poke his nose into things and stir the pot up a bit. She was probably counting on the fact that I'd stumble onto your having stayed at the Alexandria, just in case Homicide wasn't smart enough to do it themselves. And then to make sure, she slips me a story about a friend of hers seeing you outside the restaurant at the Hotel Alexandria—"

"She did?"

"Yeah. Let's face it, Lomax. She *wanted* it found out that you were in San Francisco that night."

"But why?"

I thought I was going to have to explain it to him, but suddenly a light seemed to go on in his head.

Lomax downed his glass and poured more whiskey into it. "So it was a set up from the very beginning. I've been a real chump, haven't I, Tolliver?"

"Yeah. That's one word for it. But you aren't the first guy to allow himself to be led astray by a skirt."

"But that means—"

"Yeah, Mrs. Mauston is the one who killed her husband. She may not have been the one that pulled the trigger, though I wouldn't put it past her, but she's been behind the whole thing."

"But you believe me, though, that it was a setup? That I had no part in it. You can explain it to the police, can't you?"

"I can try. They might even believe me. That is if they can find the person who really killed Mauston. And prove it in a court of law. If not, well they just may take the easy way out and prosecute the poor sap who lied about his alibi."

"What am I going to do, Tolliver? You've got to help me."

21.

"You want my advice, Lomax," I told him after taking a swig of beer, "you'll give yourself up."

"I can't do that, Tolliver. I know the way the police work. If they've got a suspect in custody, they won't go looking any farther. I turn myself in; I might as well head right to San Quentin."

"Look, if you stay here, it's only a matter of time before someone notices and calls the sheriff's office or whoever the cops are in this burg. If they come looking for you, there's a good chance it's going to end up badly. These hick law enforcement types are liable to shoot first and ask questions later, and the one thing that can be said for most of them is that they can hit what they aim at. You turn yourself in; there won't be any gunplay. Sure, you might spend some time in the jailhouse, but you'll be alive, and you'll be able to hire yourself a decent lawyer. The only real thing the cops have on you is that you lied about your alibi. They'll check that out, of course, but they'll find what I found, which is that you didn't have enough time to kill Mauston. Lt. Miller is a reasonable guy. He'll be mad because you lied to him, but he won't let that keep him from finding the truth. If you want, I can talk to him, arrange a nice safe way for you to turn yourself in, no drama, no gunplay."

"You really think that's the best thing to do, Tolliver?"

"It's the only thing to do."

"I'll think about it."

"You do that, Lomax." I took another swig of beer. It was the last of the bottle. I thought about having another, but it was a long drive back, and my head was starting to hurt again.

"What are you going to do now, Tolliver?" Lomax asked.

"Me, I'm going to head back to San Francisco."

"Are you going to tell the police where I am?"

"Only if they ask. I won't lie to you, Lomax. I'm going to look out for myself. I've got a business and a license to protect. If Miller asks me where I've been, I'm going to tell him."

He looked at me. For a second I thought he was going to get mad, and that his pistol was still resting on the bar in front of him, but he just slumped a little.

"Thanks for being straight with me, Tolliver. Have a nice drive."

We didn't bother with goodbyes.

I asked the bartender, and he said the quickest way back to Sausalito was the inland road through San Rafael, so that was the way I took. It wasn't as scenic, but it was quicker, with fewer twists and turns.

I was glad I had gotten out of there in one piece. It could have gone wrong in so many ways. Lomax had struck me as a man at the end of his tether, not sure which way to jump. I still didn't like him, but I had to feel sorry for him. I hoped that he'd take me up on my offer. I didn't want to be reading about a shootout up in Marin County in the morning paper.

It was after dark when I got back to Gene's Garage in Sausalito. It had closed for the night, but Gene was still there waiting for me. I couldn't tell if he was surprised to see the Buick back in one piece or not. Gene has got a great poker face. It's too bad he has a habit of drawing to an inside straight.

"How was the car?"

"Not bad. I might have to get me one of these after they open the bridge."

"I can make you a great deal," Gene responded.

"I'll think about it. I know I'm a little late. Did you make the call?"

"I thought I'd give you another hour. It's a long drive up to Olema and back, especially if you don't know the road. Was that alright?"

"Yeah, that was just fine," I assured him.

"Things worked out okay then?"

"As well as can be expected. Can you give me a lift to the ferry?"

"Might as well, it's on the way home."

Gene didn't ask any more questions on the way to the ferry landing. That's was one of the things I liked about him.

It was nearly ten o'clock by the time the ferry deposited me at the Hyde St. Pier in San Francisco. I was dead tired. I thought about stopping at the office, but then thought better of it and headed to my apartment. I was sound asleep by eleven.

I awoke to a pounding. At first, I thought it was my head but then realized that it was coming from the door of my apartment. Someone was banging on it. I turned over, hoping they'd go away, but that didn't work, they kept on pounding.

I realized that the only way to stop the noise would be to answer the door. When I got up, I noticed that I'd taken off my shirt and shoes, but still had on my pants. I'd been very tired.

The shirt was hanging over the back of a chair. I thought about putting it on but decided not to bother.

I yelled, "Go away. Who is it?" Not exactly coherent, but I'd just woken up.

"It's Lt. Miller. Open up, Tolliver. We need to talk." He sounded mad as a wet chicken.

I wasn't going to be able to brush him off through the door, so I opened it. Miller was standing there, his face red as a beet. There was a beefy guy standing behind him that I didn't recognize, but I could tell that he was another cop. He might be in plain clothes, but he had the look.

Miller didn't bother to say hello; he just pushed his way into the apartment. The other detective followed, shutting the door behind him.

"Make yourself at home, why don't you?" I suggested.

"This is no time to play smart guy, Tolliver. Where were you yesterday?"

"I took a drive in the country. I thought it might help to clear my head."

"Did it?" Miller barked.

"Sure. Don't I look all bright tailed and bushy eyed this morning?"

"Can it, Jim. I'm in no mood. You've been holding out on me."

"I haven't been holding out on you, Miller."

"So where were you, then?"

"I went up to meet with Lomax. I thought I might be able to get him to turn himself in."

"Did you convince him?" Miller asked, slightly mollified.

"He said he'd think about it. Look, do you mind if I make us some coffee. I haven't had anything to eat since—I guess it was breakfast in the hospital. In case you've forgotten, I suffered a serious injury recently."

Miller looked like he was going to say something about that, but then just nodded, "go ahead."

I messed around in the kitchen alcove for a few minutes, putting grounds in the percolator. I tossed a couple of pieces of bread into the toaster, too. I took my time, wanting my head to clear up. I would have liked to have fried up some eggs, but I thought that might be pushing Miller a bit too far. By the time I had buttered the toast, the coffee was ready. I found three cups and brought them and the coffee pot over to the table I use to eat on.

I sat down at the table. Miller sat across from me. His sidekick continued to stand as if he was expecting me to make a break for it.

"Who's your friend?" I asked Miller.

"This is Sergeant Jersey. He's working the Mauston case with me."

"So you've decided it's a murder case now, and not a suicide?"

"I'm keeping an open mind. Thanks to you. Now, what's the story with Lomax?"

"He called me at my office. It turns out he'd been calling me for a day or so while I was in the hospital. I guess he hadn't heard that I'd been conked on the head. Anyway, he realized that he was in a pickle because his alibi won't hold, and he wanted my help in getting him out of it. By the way, he's up in Olema, holed up in the hotel there."

"Which one?" Jersey asked.

"I'm pretty sure there's only the one."

"Olema," Miller said. "That's up near Point Reyes?"

"Yeah, that's the place. Charming little town."

"Mind if the sergeant here uses your phone?"

"Be my guest. Just no long distance, please."

Sgt. Jersey picked up the phone and made a call. I couldn't hear what he was saying, but I had a pretty good idea that he was arranging to have Lomax picked up.

"Okay, so Lomax called you. What did you do?"

"He said he wanted to talk. Face to face. So I said I would drive up there and talk to him. That's where I was yesterday."

"Why didn't you arrest him?"

"For one thing, he had a gun. For another, I'm just a *private* detective, not a cop like you. But mostly, because I don't think he's guilty of anything worse than being a dumb sap who fell for the wrong broad."

"Look, Tolliver, that's for a judge and jury to decide."

"Yeah, and I wanted to make sure that Lomax lives to let them. I'm not defending Lomax's lying to you about being in San Francisco that night. That was stupid on his part. But Lomax didn't kill Mauston. And I don't think he had any part in it either."

"How do you figure that?"

"Like I told you in the hospital, Lomax had dinner at the Hotel Alexandria around ten-thirty that night. He was on the train to Salt Lake City that left the station at 12:15. He had to finish his dinner, catch the ferry to Oakland, and catch the train. That doesn't leave much time for murder, does it?"

"Maybe Lomax killed Mauston before he had dinner at the hotel," Miller protested. "The medical examiner might be wrong about the time of death. Those kinds of things aren't exact, you know."

"Maybe. But it couldn't have been too much earlier. I've talked to someone who had dinner with Mauston that evening."

"Who?" Miller asked.

"That's neither here nor there for the moment. I'll give you her name if it becomes important. But it just means that Mauston was alive at around nine. The clerk at the hotel says Lomax went up to his room with a woman before then, maybe around eight or so, and wasn't seen until he came down for dinner."

"Are you sure about all this, Jim?"

"Sure enough. Now maybe Lomax came down without being seen and got a taxi to take him to Mauston's office, killed him and then went back to the hotel, but that seems a stretch to me. It seems more likely to me that he and his lady friend spent those couple of hours in his room, but that's just me. Of course, you can check up on all this."

"Of course," Miller responded flatly. I had to admit that it was a lot for the detective to take in all at once.

"Good. It's about time you do your job. But talk to the house dick at the hotel. And Luigi, he's the maitre d'. Oh, and the guy who was the desk clerk that night. And look in the register for Edgar Larkin. Same name he used to book the train back to Salt Lake City."

Sgt. Jersey was busy writing all this down in a little notebook. Miller was just staring at me.

"The point is, Lomax was set up to be the fall guy for Mauston's murder in case one was needed. That's why I wanted to talk to him. I wanted to find out why he gave a phony alibi."

"And did you?" Miller asked.

"Sure. It was about what I expected, too."

"Well, out with it, Tolliver. Why did he lie to us?"

"Lomax was in San Francisco that night because he had been having an affair with a married woman whose husband had gotten suspicious. She had telegraphed Lomax saying that her husband would be busy that night and she could meet him someplace. That place was the Hotel Alexandria. That's where Lomax was before he had dinner, which is why he couldn't have killed Mauston earlier. He was busy. The desk clerk at the hotel saw him meeting a woman in the hotel lobby. And the reason why Lomax wouldn't admit that he was in San Francisco that night, was because the woman had asked him not to. She didn't want her virtue compromised, or something like that."

"Did the desk clerk get a look at the woman? Can he identify her?"

"No. He said that her back was turned to him when she and Lomax met in the lobby. He didn't see her after that."

"Well, will Lomax's lady friend come forward now that he's about to be charged with murder?"

"Oh, I doubt that. I really do," I responded.

"Why is that? After all, if she doesn't, it might mean the gas chamber for Lomax."

"She won't come forward because I just happen to know who the woman is."

"Well, don't keep me in suspense. Who is she?" Miller demanded.

"She won't come forward because the woman that met Lomax that night was Helen Mauston!"

22.

"Helen Mauston? Are you sure about that, Jim?"

"That's what Lomax told me. I tend to believe him."

"But you know what the implication is, don't you?"

"I've got a pretty good idea. I'd also like to point out that Mrs. Mauston left Lomax at the Hotel Alexandria sometime before eleven. And she didn't have to catch the late train to Salt Lake City."

Miller looked at me, his eyes widening as he put all the information together.

"But she said that she was home that night," Miller protested. "Her maid backs up her story."

"Interesting, isn't it?" I commented.

"Yeah, that's one word for it. What proof do you have for any of this, Jim?"

"So far, I've only got Lomax's word for it. I'm not sure how much that would be worth in a court. It certainly isn't going to be enough for the prosecutor."

"It doesn't make sense, Jim. We were ready to close the case as a suicide. Why would Mrs. Mauston want to hire a private detective to stir things up? It seems pretty risky to me."

"It all comes back to that insurance policy, Miller. A quarter of a million dollars would convince a lot of people to take a risk. The way I have it figured, she might not have known about the suicide clause in the policy when she killed her husband, so when she finds out she can't collect if Mauston's death is ruled a suicide, she hires me. But from the start, she'd had a plan B with Lomax set up as the fall guy. Pretty clever when you come to think about it. She lures Lomax into San Francisco that night and then gets him to lie about it knowing that if the police get wind of the fact that his alibi is phony, he'd become the number one suspect leaving her in the clear. She's probably hoping that Lomax will resist arrest and end up getting himself killed by the police. You know that's the way these things work. And with a dead patsy to pin the case on, the prosecutor might not bother to look much further."

"You really think Mauston's wife killed him? That she's capable of premeditated murder?"

"You haven't looked into her cold, green eyes, lieutenant. I think that woman is capable of almost anything if she thinks that the reward is great enough."

I admit that it was a lot to take in. Miller still had some old-fashioned notions about women. I didn't.

"Look, Miller, it all fits. She had the opportunity to do it. She left the Hotel Alexandria before eleven. It wouldn't have taken her more than a half-hour to get to Mauston's office. She's one person that Mauston would have let up into his office without giving it a second thought. He probably wouldn't have been on his guard, either. She pulls the pistol, and remember it was hers, she pulls it out of her handbag when he isn't looking and pops him one in the head at close range. Then she leaves it laying on the desk to make it look like a suicide."

"We didn't find any fingerprints," Miller objected.

"She was probably wearing gloves. Women do that, you know."

"Okay. Say that what you just described to me is true. What do you expect me to do about it?"

"For a start, you might see if you can find a witness that can place her at the hotel. Or one that saw her coming or going from Far Eastern Specialties. That might not be that hard. A good-looking woman in that part of town after midnight. She'd attract attention. That's what you probably should have done in the first place instead of assuming it was a suicide."

"Don't rub it in, Tolliver. You aren't in the clear yourself. You've been hiding a fugitive—"

"I wasn't hiding him; he was managing that all by himself."

"Okay, but technically you're still working for Mrs. Mauston."

"Yeah, and she hired me to find her husband's killer. That's what I'm doing," I replied grimly.

"Even if she's the one that did it?"

"Even if she's the one," I stated. "Look, Miller, why don't you get out of here and let me have my breakfast. I haven't had anything to eat in the last twenty-four hours except two slices of toast and a couple of warm beers. Go find yourself some witnesses. Go arrest Lomax and put him someplace where he'll be safe from himself. Go talk to the widow and see how she reacts. Just get out of here and let me get dressed."

"Alright, alright. I'll get out of your hair, but you hear anything, you let me know, understand? No more traipsing up to Olema or wherever without telling me first."

"Sure thing, Miller," I agreed cheerily as I showed him to the door.

It was a little after noon that I got to the office. I'd had time to wrap myself around a pair of fried eggs, take a shower, and change my clothes. I'd fiddle with the bandage and decided that my head wouldn't fall off if I removed it. I still had to be careful when I put my hat on, but I'd be okay.

Miller had asked a good question. I knew that Mrs. Mauston had killed her husband, but what was I going to do about it? The police would probably have better luck than I would tracking down witnesses that had seen her that night, so I'd leave that to them. There didn't seem much else to do for the moment.

On a hunch, I called Florence Bouchet.

"James, it's so good to hear from you." The way she said it made me think it might be true.

"Hi, Florence. I've got a question that you might be able to help me with. Do you know who has keys to Far Eastern's offices?"

"I'm not sure. Mr. Mauston and Mr. Nilgren. I don't think any of the other staff would have had one. Oh, and Mr. Lomax, of course."

"What about Mrs. Mauston?"

"No, I don't think so, but I can't be sure," she said uncertainly.

"Thanks, Florence. You've been a big help. I'll give you a call."

"You do that James. Good-bye."

It probably wasn't important. Mrs. Mauston might have been able to make a duplicate of her husband's key. She also might have lifted Lomax's. She would have had a chance to do that while they were in the room at the Hotel Alexandria. I'd have to ask Lomax about that if he called.

I was kind of hoping that he *would* call saying that he was ready to turn himself in. That's why I jumped when the phone rang. It wasn't Lomax, though, it was Miller.

"Lomax was gone when the sheriff finally got around to going up to Olema. The hotel manager said that he must have left sometime in the middle of the night. His car was gone in the morning, and no one saw him leave. You haven't heard from him, have you, Tolliver?"

"No. In fact, I was sitting here hoping he'd call."

Miller grunted. "I went around and had a talk with the widow."

"How'd that go?"

"About as you'd expect. At first, she tried to flirt with me. She does a damn good job of that. When she saw I wasn't biting, she clammed up. I see what you meant about those damned green eyes of hers, though. They can chill a man to the bone."

"Mrs. Miller will be proud of you, lieutenant."

"Yeah, except I won't mention it to her. You let me know if you hear anything."

The line went dead before I could respond.

About a half-hour after that, the phone rang again. It wasn't Lomax; it was Mrs. Mauston.

"James, we need to talk." She didn't sound desperate, but she was pleading.

"What about, Helen?"

"The police were here, James. Questioning me. That Lt. Miller. He seems to have gotten the idea into his head that I was somehow responsible for Charles's death. I'm worried. Can you come over here as soon as possible?"

I thought about it for a second. Did I really want to go into the black widow's den? But then, it might be the only way to get at the truth.

"Jim? I need your help, please." The pleading note of the poor widow was in her voice, the same voice she had used that first time in my office.

"Sure, Helen. I can be there in a half hour or so. Will that be alright?"

"That would be fine, Jim. But hurry." She didn't say good-bye.

I called Homicide trying to reach Miller, but he wasn't in, so I left a message for him:

"Mrs. Mauston just asked that I come to her apartment, so I'm going now. I thought you'd want to know."

Out of habit, I checked the .38 automatic in my shoulder holster, and then gingerly put on my hat. Down on the street, I hailed a cab and headed to the Mauston residence.

Ada met me at the door. As she took my hat, I noticed how muscular her arms were, no doubt her upbringing as a farm girl. They were strong arms, strong enough to have struck the blow that had knocked me out. Had Mrs. Mauston really told her she could to go to bed that night, or had she told her to wait in the street below to bash my brains in? It was something to think about. If Ada was willing to lie for her mistress, she might have been willing to kill for her. Two-hundred and fifty grand split two ways is still a lot of cash.

"Mrs. Mauston is expecting you."

"Thanks."

Mrs. Mauston was waiting in the living room. She was wearing a silky pair of what I think are described as lounging pajamas. I hadn't thought women actually wore them outside of the movies. I had to admit that they looked good on her.

"Jim, what happened to your head?" she asked innocently. I'd taken off the bandage, but there was still a bald patch where they'd shaved it before putting in some stitches.

"Somebody tried to use my head for batting practice outside your apartment the other night."

"How terrible. Why don't the police do something about things like that rather than harass poor widows like me?"

"You'll have to take that up with city hall, Mrs. Mauston."

"Mrs. Mauston? I thought we had agreed on more familiar terms."

"I thought that seeing as we were going to be talking business I'd keep it more professional."

"I see. Very well. As I said, that Lt. Miller was here. He had a lot of questions about where I was the night Charles was killed. He implied that I had been in a hotel room with Edward Lomax. Where could he have gotten such an idea?"

"Probably from Lomax."

That seemed to surprise her for a moment.

"Then they've arrested him?"

"Not yet."

"I don't understand, Jim."

"It's like this. The police haven't talked to Lomax yet, but I have. Yesterday, at a place up the coast. We had a pretty interesting discussion over drinks."

"Oh, about what?"

"About a number of things, but mostly about how he came to be at the Hotel Alexandria that night. It turns out it hadn't been his idea. He said that you had suggested it."

"What are you implying, Jim?"

"Oh, I'm not implying anything, Helen. But Lomax has got this crazy idea in his head that he was set up to be the fall guy for your husband's death."

"I'm afraid Edward must be deranged. What other explanation can there be? First, he kills Charles, and then he has this delusion that I was with him at a hotel that night. Ada will testify that I was here at home all that night."

"I'm sure she will."

"Don't you believe me, Jim?"

In her own way, Mrs. Mauston was a pretty good actress. She might fool some people. She might even fool a jury.

"You can try and argue it that way, Helen. Who knows, you might even be able to get away with it. That is unless the police can find a witness to back up Lomax's story."

"Do you think they can do that?" she asked alarmed.

"Maybe. You are a rather striking woman, Helen. The kind people tend to remember. Someone may have seen you in the hotel lobby. Or on the way to Far Eastern's office. Maybe a cab driver or something. Or didn't you take a taxi? Do you own a car, Helen? Can you drive? What about your maid, Ada? Can she drive? I'm pretty sure she can do some other things."

"I'm not sure that I like your tone, Jim."

"I get that a lot, you know. Something about my voice, I guess. It gets on people's nerves, especially when I start talking about things they'd rather leave unsaid."

She looked at me with those calculating green eyes of hers trying to decide the best way to twist me around those long, elegant fingers of hers. I was afraid she might find one.

"I admit it, Jim. I'm in a real mess. It's partly my fault, too. I should never have encouraged Edward. He must have thought that if Charles was dead, that he could have me to himself. And now the police are going to put the worst possible interpretation on things and assume that the two of us were in some sort of conspiracy together to kill my husband and split the insurance money. Even though I had nothing to do with Charles's death."

"That's certainly possible, Helen. The police don't always have a lot of imagination in these matters. They tend to pick the simplest explanations. And I'm sure that a lot of people, looking at the evidence, might think your husband's death was something the two of you cooked up between you. That's the way they'd write it up in a mystery book."

"But you can't believe that, can you, Jim? You can't think me capable of murdering my own husband?" She was putting just the right hysterical pitch into her voice. If she did that in a courtroom, she just *might* convince a jury.

I tried to bring her down to earth. "Let's just say I'm keeping an open mind for now."

"Oh, Jim! What am I going to do? You've got to help me. You're the only one who can."

23.

I was puzzled by Mrs. Mauston's request. Did she really believe that I still thought she was innocent of her husband's death? Was she delusional on the subject? Or was it just a façade she was presenting so as not to admit her crime? I didn't know, and I wasn't sure I cared.

"I'm not exactly sure what you think I can do, Helen?"

"I would have thought that was obvious, Jim. The police won't be satisfied until they have someone that they can prosecute for the murder. What we need to do is to provide them with that someone. They already suspect Edward. You said that they've issued a warrant or whatever for his arrest. Well, all we have to do is convince them that they've made the right choice."

"Let me get this straight, Helen. You want me to shade the evidence so that Lomax looks guilty. Is that about the size of it?"

"You make it sound so horrible, Jim."

"But that's what we're talking about, aren't we? Right now, the police aren't sure about Lomax. But if they become convinced that he killed Mauston, they might not be so careful when they arrest him. The last time I talked to him, he didn't sound particularly stable. There's no telling what he might do if he finds himself surrounded. It could end up badly. Lomax could end up dead."

"Would that be so bad, Jim?" she asked. The way she said it sent a chill through me. "If Lomax were to be killed by the police, they won't be eager to admit that they might have made a mistake. It might be for the best all around. The police could close their case. There wouldn't be any trial that might go the wrong way. The insurance company would have to pay out. Everybody would be happier."

"Except for Lomax. He'd be dead. Of course, he couldn't complain then, could he? Or implicate anyone else, either?"

"Yes, there is that, Jim. But as I said, it might be for the best."

I was having trouble keeping a straight face. I've run across some bad people in my line of work, some that you might even call evil, but I couldn't remember anyone that had been so casually amoral.

"Has it occurred to you that Lomax might be innocent?"

"Does that matter, Jim? What's Lomax to you? He's not your friend. He's not your client. What can he offer you? You can't even be absolutely sure that he didn't commit the murder. Why should he be the one to go free and I go to prison?"

"Well, seeing as you put it that way—"

"Just think about it, Jim. If Lomax is convicted, the insurance company will be forced to pay on the policy." The excited edge was back in her voice. Not hysteria, but something darker and more twisted. Behind that beautiful face, I was seeing something that was no longer quite human. "Two-hundred and fifty thousand dollars, Jim. That's a lot of money, and some of it could be yours."

I decided to play along for a moment to see just how far she'd go.

"Just how much are we talking about?"

That seemed to stop her for a moment.

"I don't understand, Jim."

"I mean, just what would my cut be? Fifty grand? A hundred? Half of the two-hundred and fifty? After all, you *are* asking me to commit perjury."

"Why, Jim. I thought that we would share it. With that much money, we could go off somewhere and live in luxury, just the two of us."

"That's a very tempting offer, Helen. There's not many dames that have offered me a share of both a quarter of a million and themselves. The thing is, you haven't had such a great track record with the men in your life lately. After all, your husband is dead, and you are about to sell Lomax down the river. How long would it be before you decided to get rid of me?"

"How can you ask that, Jim? It would be different with you. Charles was an old man. And Edward? We both know what kind of man Edward is. Neither one of them was half the man you are."

It was all starting to sound like the dialog from a movie. Perhaps that was where she had picked it up.

"That may be, Helen. I won't argue the point. But I don't believe in taking chances. Let's face it; it might not work out for us. I'd prefer to have some cash up front that I could sock away for a rainy day, so just how much of that two-hundred and fifty G's are you willing to part with?"

"You make it sound so crass, Jim." She almost managed to sound indignant.

"I guess I'm just kind of a crass person."

She paused, the calculator behind those cold green eyes crunching sums.

"I suppose that I could give you twenty thousand. Once the insurance company pays out. As a fee for your services. Will that make you happy, Jim?"

"I was thinking more along the lines of fifty thousand. And I'd have to have some of it now. After all, I'm taking a big risk. The police might not bite. They just might decide that Lomax is innocent no matter what I tell them. I'll need a little insurance of my own before I commit myself. Say ten thousand dollars."

"But, Jim, I don't have that sort of ready money available. I had no money of my own, just an allowance from Charles. I couldn't possibly come up with ten thousand dollars."

"There must be some way. You've got jewelry or things that you could pawn. That necklace you're wearing must be worth at least ten grand."

"You can't possibly ask me to sell some of my jewelry."

"Look, I don't care how you raise the money, Helen. That's your business. But I'm not going to frame a man unless I have some hard cash in hand. That's my business."

"I misjudged you. You're not the man I thought you were, Mr. Tolliver."

"No, I don't think I am, Helen. It's too bad, but that's the way it is. I don't particularly like Lomax, but I happen to believe that he's innocent, and I can't see myself framing him for a murder he didn't commit. Not for you and not for fifty thousand dollars."

Mrs. Mauston had wandered over to the sideboard where there was a cigarette case and a lighter. She turned away as if to pick up a cigarette, but when she turned back, there was a small, silver automatic in her hand. It was pointed at me. It looked like it was only a .32, but at that close range, the caliber wouldn't really make a difference.

"That's too bad, Jim. I had been counting on you. I had thought that we could come to an understanding, but I can see now I was mistaken."

"I guess we both were."

She didn't respond, and the pistol was still pointed at my chest.

"You know, Helen, there's been something that's been puzzling me. Why did you choose to hire a private detective in the first place?"

"Because, to get the insurance I had to prove that Charles's death wasn't a suicide. That was a mistake on my part. I should have read the policy more carefully before—well, I only discovered that clause afterward when that insurance man, Mandelbrot, pointed it out. The police seemed to have satisfied themselves that it was a suicide. Obviously, the insurance company was happy with their conclusion. I needed someone to shake things up."

"I understand that, but why did you hire me in particular? I'm not the only private investigator in San Francisco. Why not someone else? Why not one of the big agencies?"

"Because I wanted someone that would be successful, but not too successful. I needed someone who would create enough doubt so that the insurance company would be forced to pay out, but who wouldn't actually be able to discover what really had happened."

"So you settled on me," I said sarcastically.

"Well, yes. A one-man operation, not much of a reputation, not many resources. I thought you would be ideal. Unfortunately, it seems I underestimated you."

"If you like I can refer you to someone else. I hear Lance Donovan is flexible in the ethics department."

"It's a little too late for that now. I doubt if he has your sense of humor, though, Jim. That was one of the things that I liked about you."

"Were there others?"

"Not really. Let's not kid ourselves, Jim. Ours was always going to be just a business relationship."

"So what happens now, Helen?"

"I'm afraid that I'll have to terminate our relationship." The pistol in her hand wavered just slightly.

She called out in a louder voice, "Ada, can you come in here a moment?"

The maid must have been waiting just outside the living room because she appeared almost immediately.

"Ada, would you please relieve Mr. Tolliver of the pistol he's carrying under his jacket?"

The maid reached around under my jacket for my automatic, being careful to not to put herself in the line of fire. She stepped back out of reach, holding the pistol as if she knew how to use it.

"Out of curiosity, what's Ada's cut of the insurance money?

"Ada knows that I'll take care of her. I always have." A smile cracked the maid's broad prairie face.

"So, which one of you ladies pulled the trigger? Was it you Helen, or the Swede here?"

"Oh, I had that pleasure, Jim. You don't know how tiresome Charles had become these last few years. I was happy to shoot him."

"How'd you manage that so easy?"

"It was easy. I knew Charles would be there alone. He'd told me himself. I'd taken Edward's key to the office when we were in the hotel. Charles never heard me as I went up the stairs. You should have seen the look of surprise on his face when he looked up and saw me standing there almost next to him with the pistol in my hand. I shot him before he could react. After I had done it, I pressed his hand around the handle of the gun and left it laying on his desk. Then I let myself out, locking the door behind me. I was going to sneak the key back on Edwards key ring, but I never had a chance. Ada just drove the car."

"Did you know what you are getting yourself into, Ada?" I asked the maid.

"Ya. I knew," she answered flatly.

"It was Ada that hit you over the head the other night," Helen said, almost proudly.

"Yeah, I kind of figured that one out by myself."

"Anyway, Ada picked me up at the hotel and drove me home to pick up the pistol—"

"I was wondering about, Helen. That had me confused. I knew that you left the hotel before ten-thirty, and I knew that Mauston hadn't been killed until after midnight. I couldn't quite figure out what you were doing in the time between. After all, it would only have taken fifteen or twenty minutes at the most to drive from the hotel to the office. I had thought that maybe you needed the time to work up the nerve, but, somehow, I don't think that was a problem with you."

"If you must know, Jim, I didn't take the pistol to the hotel with me because I didn't want to risk it being seen by Edward. That would have been unfortunate. He might actually have tried to stop me. So Ada drove me home, I got the pistol, and then we drove to the office, and then when it was done, she drove me home. That's why there won't be any taxi drivers that recognized me that night. You see, I thought of everything, Jim."

"Except for reading the insurance policy."

"I suppose one *can't* think of everything. There are times one must improvise."

"Won't my demise raise some awkward questions?"

"Undoubtedly. I'll have to think of something to tell the police. Perhaps I mistook you for a burglar. No, better yet, I'll tell them I thought you were Edward. That I fired in the dark and didn't see that it was you."

"It's not dark yet, Helen. It doesn't get dark this time of year till after eight."

"I'll guess we'll just have to wait until then. Why don't you sit down, Jim? It will be more comfortable. For both of us."

"If it's all the same to you, I'll stand."

"I really would prefer it if you sat." The pistol in her hand gestured emphatically.

I took a seat on the sofa. I was wondering if Miller had gotten my message, and if he had, would he choose to act on it.

"So what was Lomax's role in this whole thing? Was he just a dupe?"

"You're just full of questions, aren't you? Even now."

"As you said, we've got time on our hands until you pull the trigger, why not spend it in conversation."

"You *are* amusing, Jim. Edward was to be *my* insurance policy. In case the police investigation came too close. If it did, I could always drop a hint that Edward's alibi was a lie. They'd investigate, as you did, and discover that he had been in San Francisco that night. I had thought that that would be enough to throw suspicion on him."

"So that was all your idea?"

"Oh, yes. The whole thing. His coming to San Francisco, registering at the hotel under an assumed name, taking the night train back to Salt Lake City. I wanted it to be hard enough to discover so that it would all appear believable when it came out. And, of course, I told Edward to keep it a secret to protect my virtue."

"That was a nice touch. The poor sap."

"Yes, poor Edward. He really always did think he was more charming than he actually was. But men are often like that, don't you think?"

"I suspect you're right, Helen. Speaking of him, I wonder where Lomax is right now?"

"With any luck, the police will have caught him—or killed him."

We were interrupted by the doorbell. I was hoping it was Miller.

"Ada, would you go and answer that. Send whoever it is away. Tell them I'm out or something. Oh, and you'd better leave the gun somewhere out of Mr. Tolliver's reach."

The maid set my pistol down on a lamp table far enough away that I'd never have a chance to get to it. She disappeared into the hallway. We could hear the sound of the door being opened and then there was a thud as if the door had been forced back. A few seconds later Ada backed into the living room, followed by Lomax who was holding a gun in his hand.

24.

"Welcome to the party, Lomax," I said cheerfully. "Things were just getting interesting. Helen has just been telling me how she played you for a sap. Don't feel bad, though; I think she has been planning to do the same for me."

He took in the scene, his eyes darting from me to Mrs. Mauston to the gun in her hand. He looked like a man who had had too many drinks and not enough sleep over the past week. He hadn't shaved in a couple of days or changed his clothes, either. There was just a hint of a shake to the hand that held the gun.

"You, over there," he ordered the maid, pointing to a chair in the corner. Ada looked towards her mistress who just nodded. The maid went over and sat in the chair, and watched the room from her placid Scandinavian face.

"What's been going on here?" demanded.

"Mrs. Mauston has been trying to sell you out, Lomax. She wants my help in making you the patsy for your partner's murder. A very tempting offer, too, though we were still dickering about the terms."

"You were going to double-cross me, Tolliver?"

"Do you see me holding a gun, Lomax? I declined the offer. Helen and I couldn't come to an agreement. We were just discussing the termination of our business relationship when you walked in."

"Your banter is getting boring, Jim," Mrs. Mauston said nervously.

"Earlier you said you found it amusing."

"I lied."

"Yes, that seems to be a habit with you. You lead men on and then offer them up as sacrifices." I turned to Lomax, "She offered herself up to me if I would convince the police that you were the guilty party. She even hinted that it would be better if the police didn't take you alive. Save the possibility of an embarrassing trial."

"Why don't you just shut up?" Helen cried.

"Oh, let him talk, Helen," Lomax said. "I'm interested in what he has to say. I'd like to learn just how much of a sap I've been."

"Yeah, Helen. Why don't you put down the gun and have a seat? We can talk this over like old friends."

Whether by luck or instinct, Lomax had positioned himself so that Mrs. Mauston couldn't easily cover the two of us. She was licking her lips trying to decide which of us was the biggest threat.

"I've got an idea," I said. "Why don't I pick up that pistol laying over on the table there and then we'll have the makings of a real proper Mexican standoff."

"I don't think that would be such good idea, Tolliver," Lomax said.

"Have it your way," I shrugged.

I slumped back into the sofa. I wondered how long the situation could last. Both Lomax and Mrs. Mauston were looking as if the tension was getting to them. It was only a matter of time before one or the other of them broke.

"What should I do, Tolliver?" Lomax asked, his voice quavering just a little.

"The smart thing, Lomax, would be for you to let me pick up my gun and call the police. What I've heard tonight should be more than enough to clear you of Mauston's murder."

"Just what did you hear?"

"It's quite a story, Lomax. Ada over there picked up Mrs. Mauston at the hotel after she left you and drove her to Far Eastern's office. Then she waited outside in the car while Mrs. Mauston went up and shot her husband. After that, she drove Mrs. Mauston home. Of course, she was lying when she told the police that the two of them were home all night, but what's a little perjury compared to being an accessory to murder?"

I glanced over at the maid, but if my little speech had made any impression on her, it wasn't showing.

"And where do I fit in to all this?" Lomax asked. "Why did Helen insist that I come to San Francisco that night? Why did she have to drag me into this mess?"

"It might be a blow to your ego, Lomax, but you were just the backup plan. You were a patsy to fall back on if the cops got too curious. Of course, if Helen here had read the insurance policy beforehand, she might have set you up to take the fall from the beginning, but she didn't. So when she found out they don't pay out for suicides, she needed a murderer. You got elected. It was Helen here that put me onto the fact that you'd booked into the Hotel Alexandria that night."

"Really, I wish you'd just shut up, Jim," Helen said.

"You said that before, Helen. I guess I just talk too much. Of course, if Lomax here ends up the fall guy, he at least deserves to know why. I think it's only fair, don't you?"

I wondered just how far I should take needling the two of them. I felt like I was holding a bottle of nitro-glycerin on a bumpy road. I was playing for time, but I had a feeling that time was running out.

"You know, Edward, maybe we can still work this out," Helen said, her voice suddenly smooth and seductive. "Maybe we can set this up so that Tolliver takes the blame for Charles's murder."

"Just how would that work, Helen?" Lomax asked skeptically.

"Yes, how *would* that work, Helen?" I asked, trying to be helpful.

"We could say that he had been blackmailing me. That he'd found out about our affair and threatened to expose us. Then, when we said we couldn't get the money, he came up with a scheme to murder Charles for the insurance money. After he killed him, he said that he would reveal our affair to the police and make it look like we were the ones who had killed Charles unless I turned over the insurance settlement."

"See," I interjected. "A moment ago she was all set to send you to the gas chamber and split the proceeds with me, but now she's perfectly willing to do things the other way around. What's the saying, 'Fickle, thy name is woman' or some such?"

"Shut up, Jim, or I'll shut you up," Mrs. Mauston said waving the gun in her hand menacingly in my direction.

I could see Lomax trying to decide between what he wished for and what he knew was the truth. "You don't really think you could get away with that, do you, Helen?"

"Why not? With your help, I'm sure we could convince the police that Tolliver planned the whole thing from the beginning. After all, it's nearly the truth. He's been trying to manipulate the situation for his benefit. He came here tonight with the intention of seducing me into agreeing to his plan. It was all his idea to frame you for the murder."

"Don't listen to her, Lomax. Remember that before you got here, she was trying to shop the same deal to me, except that you were going to be the guy on the short end of the stick. How long do you think it would be before you ended up like me—or her husband?"

"Edward, think about it," Mrs. Mauston said, honey dripping from her words. "We could kill him right here. We could say he threatened us when we wouldn't pay blackmail. That's his pistol on the table. We could claim that he was threatening me with it when you arrived and you shot him to defend me. With Tolliver dead, there would be no one to contradict our story. Ada will back up whatever we say. With three witnesses, the police will be only too glad to hang Charles's murder on him."

For a second, Lomax looked as if he were wavering. His blood-shot eyes glanced over to me and then back to Helen.

"That's the difference between you and me, Helen. I'm not a murderer. I couldn't kill someone like that. Not in cold blood. Not the way you killed Charles. I should have seen it from the beginning, but I was a fool."

"You know you were never much of anything, Edward, despite what you may have thought of yourself," Mrs. Mauston said disdainfully. "Just a slick pretty boy who could dance well. That's all you were to me, Edward."

"And you aren't half the woman you think you are, Helen," Lomax retorted. "Charles realized that, finally. I should have too. You know that he was having an affair, don't you?"

"Charles? All he cared about was his business."

"That's not true. He was having an affair with Florence Bouchet, had been for some time, Helen." Lomax was trying to rub it in. It was like striking a match on a stick of dynamite.

"That Chinese half-breed that works in the shop?" Helen spit.

"Yes. One and the same. I think she must have offered Charles the one thing you were incapable of, Helen. Honesty."

"You're lying, Edward. You're making it up to get at me."

"Ask Tolliver, here. He'll back me up."

"Hey you two, leave me out of your lover's spat," I commented. The way their emotions were peaking, I wanted their attention focused on each other, not me.

"I've had enough of you, Helen," Lomax continued. "You think you can twist every man that you run into around your little finger. Maybe you could do that at one time, but you're not so young and attractive anymore, Helen. You couldn't do it with Tolliver here, and you can't do it with me anymore, either."

The situation was getting ready to blow. Mrs. Mauston was close to the edge, and I could see that Lomax was tensing up, getting ready to pull the trigger.

"Don't do it, Lomax," I admonished. "She's not worth it." All I wanted was to give Miller time to get there before the shooting started.

"She's ruined my life, Tolliver," Lomax said pleadingly. "She killed my partner. She's made me a wanted man. You have to admit that she deserves to die."

"That's a job for the state, Lomax. You were right when you said you weren't a murderer." I'd half risen from the sofa, ready to stop him if I could. Out of the corner of my eye, I saw Helen. I could tell that she was getting ready to fire. I'd never be able to get to her in time, so I dove at Lomax.

There was a crack that echoed throughout the apartment.

25.

I'd tackled Lomax just in time; the shot had taken him in the upper part of his arm. If I'd been a fraction of a second slower, the slug would have gone through his heart.

There was a scramble as Lomax, and I hit the floor. When I came up, his gun was in my hand, pointed at Mrs. Mauston.

"Drop the pistol, Helen."

There was a vacant sparkle in her ice-green eyes, as if she were looking into some alternate reality, but she still held onto the automatic, aiming it at a point between where I stood and where Lomax lay.

"Don't you see, Jim," Mrs. Mauston said. Her voice was sultry, but now there was a tinge of madness in it. "This is our chance. We can say Lomax broke in here and held us both at gunpoint. I managed to get a gun and shot in self-defense. We could kill him now, and the police would never be any the wiser."

"Which one of us gets to finish him off?" I queried.

"Why, I thought that you could do it, Jim. That way I'd know that I would be able to trust you."

I couldn't tell if she really believed that I'd go along with a deal like that or if she was just waiting to catch me off guard so she could shoot me in the back. Either way, I wasn't having any of it.

"Put the gun down, Helen, or I'll shoot. You know I'll do it."

There was a second then when I thought I'd have to fire, but then she lowered her arm.

"Alright, Jim. You win." Mrs. Mauston set the pistol down on the sideboard next to the drinks tray.

While this exchange was going on the maid had started to stand. I pointed the gun in her direction.

"Sit down, Ada. As it is, you're only an accessory. With luck, you might only get ten or twelve years. But you interfere now, and it'll be life or worse."

The maid sat back down defiantly.

I looked over at Lomax. He'd managed to prop himself up so that his back was against an armchair. There was a stain of blood forming on the sleeve of his jacket, and his face had gone white from shock, but it looked as though he would survive for a while without attention.

"How are you doing, Lomax?" I asked encouragingly.

"It hurts, Tolliver. I didn't think it would hurt so much."

"Yeah, gunshots do that. Sorry about that. Just hang in there, Lomax. I'm going to call for help. It shouldn't take long for them to get here." I pulled out my handkerchief with my left hand and tossed it to him. "Press that against the wound. It'll help to stop the bleeding."

Lomax stared at the white square of linen for a second and then did as I had told him.

I turned my focus back to Mrs. Mauston. She had been watching me with those frozen eyes while I had talked to Lomax. Now she was readying herself for one last try.

"Think about it, Jim. You'll never have a chance like this again," she said. There was pleading in her eyes, but they were still the same frozen green. "You and me and all that money. We can go anywhere, do anything. All we have to do is shoot Edward and tell the police a story about how he broke in here, and I shot him in self-defense."

"And what about your husband? Did you shoot him in self-defense, too? The police are onto you, Helen. They're going to be asking questions. Trying to pin it on Lomax won't work any longer. Miller will decide for himself that Lomax didn't have time to kill your husband and still make the train back to Utah. You might have been able to sell that story if he hadn't been hungry and hadn't decided to have dinner at the hotel before catching the train, but the fact is that he did have that dinner and there are witnesses to back up his alibi."

"But will the police care, Jim? If they have someone to blame? Someone who's already dead?"

"Some of them will, Helen. Miller will."

There was a groan from the floor. Lomax looked as though he was about to pass out.

"Take it easy, Lomax. Sure you've been shot, but I don't think it's too bad. Just don't move around too much. I'll try to get some help here as soon as I can."

"Jim, just think about what could have been," Helen pleaded.

"I have, Helen. But it wouldn't have worked. Sooner or later the money would have come between us, and I've seen what happens to the men in your life who get in your way. It's over. I'm going to call the police now, Helen, so just stand there and don't move. If you do, I'll have to shoot you."

The phone was on a little table near the hallway. I picked up the receiver and dialed the operator.

"Connect me to the police. Homicide. Lt. Miller if you can."

It took some time while the operator made the connection. The voice on the other end wasn't Miller's.

"Who is this?"

"This is Sgt. Jersey. Who is this?"

"Tolliver. I'm at Mrs. Mauston's apartment." I gave the address. "Lomax is here. He's been shot. If you can't find Miller, you'd better come yourself. If you can't, send a couple of detectives. I've got Mrs. Mauston here, and she's confessed to killing her husband. Better send an ambulance as well."

"Just what's going on, Tolliver?" Jersey demanded.

"I just told you. I've solved the Mauston case for you. Now get Miller here as quick as you can."

I didn't want to take my attention off of Mrs. Mauston, so I hung up the phone.

As an afterthought, I dialed the *Chronicle* and asked for Floyd Packard. It had occurred to me that it might not be a bad idea to have the press on my side when the story hit the papers.

"What's up, Tolliver?" Packard asked when I was put through.

"I promised you a scoop, Floyd. Well, here it is. I'm in Mrs. Mauston's apartment. She's the one who killed her husband. She's just shot Lomax, and I'm holding a gun on her. The cops should be arriving any minute, but if you hurry, you just might beat them."

"You aren't fooling around about this, are you, Jimmy? This ain't no April Fool's prank, is it?"

"It's August, Floyd. Look, I'm kind of busy right now. I'm holding a gun on the Mauston dame, so I'm going to have to hang up on you, but if you get down here quick enough, you've got yourself a chance for some real front page pictures."

I hung the phone up before he could respond.

"There's still time, Jim. Before the police get here. Shoot Edward."

"Didn't you hear me on the phone, Helen? I told Sgt. Jersey that you'd confessed."

"We can tell them that Edward made you say that. That he held a gun on you while you made the call. We can say that he was going to kill us both and make up a story about how I was the one that had killed Charles."

"But you *did* kill Charles. Or have you forgotten that part, Helen?"

I could see that Mrs. Mauston's grip on reality was slipping away. I was starting to wonder how firm it had ever been. All her life she had twisted and manipulated men to get her way. Was she now trying to manipulate her own memories? Whether that was true or not, she was in a dangerous state of mind. I should have recognized that, but I didn't.

"It's no good, Helen. Lt. Miller is going to be here in a few minutes, and then I'm going to tell him what really happened that night, or at least what I know of it, which will be enough. You may have gotten away with adjusting things to suit your needs, but you won't be able to do that anymore, Helen—"

I was cut short by a pounding at the door.

"Police. Open up. This is Lt. Miller of Homicide."

I'd turned my head at the pounding. When I turned back, Mrs. Mauston had a gun in her hand, the one she had shot Lomax with.

"Drop it, Helen. It's no good. It's over."

"You've ruined everything, Jim. I would have been rich and free, and you could have had part of it. But you had to go and play the damned two-bit detective and spoil everything."

"Drop the gun, Helen. I'll shoot if I have to."

Outside in the hallway, I could hear the sound of beefy bodies bouncing against the apartment door. Helen's gun was up and pointed at my head. There were ten feet between us. At that distance, she couldn't miss. Neither could I. I fired.

26.

When it was over, I was still standing. Mrs. Mauston wasn't. I'm not sure if she ever got off a shot. If she did, the police never recovered the slug.

A moment after I had fired, Lt. Miller and his men managed to break through the front door. They charged in with guns drawn ready to take on everything in sight. What they found was a wounded man propped up against a chair and a wounded woman laying on the floor. Ada, the maid, hadn't moved from the chair where she'd been sitting. Me, I was the only one standing, holding a smoking gun in my hand. I can only imagine what it must have looked like. I let Sgt. Jersey pry the weapon out of my fingers. I didn't resist.

"Right in the nick of time, as usual, Miller," I remarked despite the fact that I was shaking.

"I don't need any of your wisecracks, Tolliver. What happened?"

"Do you want the long version or just a synopsis?"

"Cut to the chase, Jim. Why are there two people with gunshot wounds?"

"Speaking of which, I think Lomax there will be alright, but he could probably use some medical attention. I'm not so sure about Mrs. Mauston. I told the sergeant here to send along an ambulance—"

I was interrupted by the sound of a clanging bell as the ambulance pulled up in front of the building.

"Well, at least one thing seems to have gone right."

"Can it, Jim," Miller spat. "Who shot who? I see three guns laying around."

"One's mine, one belongs to Lomax, and the other one Mrs. Mauston had in a drawer in the sideboard there. Mrs. Mauston shot Lomax, and I shot her when she was going to shoot me just as you broke in the door. I don't know if she got off a shot at the end or not."

Sgt. Jersey went over and picked up the gun Mrs. Mauston had dropped, using a handkerchief so as not to smudge any fingerprints. Not that that mattered anymore. He held the barrel to his nose and gave a sniff.

"This one's been fired recently, lieutenant," he said as he laid the pistol down where he'd found it.

"You needn't bother smelling mine, sergeant, I freely admit that I fired a shot."

"You seem to have created quite a mess for yourself, Tolliver," Miller said shaking his head.

The ambulance crew had come up while we were talking. They gave Lomax a quick look and then went to check on Mrs. Mauston.

"She's alive, lieutenant, but we'd better get her to a hospital as soon as we can. The other feller needs to be patched up, but he's in no immediate danger. He can ride along in the ambulance if that's okay."

"Yeah, get 'em both out of here. I'll send along a couple of men. Neither one is to leave the hospital without my say so, understand."

The ambulance man just nodded. They unrolled the stretcher and got Mrs. Mauston onto it as gently as they could. It took a couple of minutes before they were out of there and I could resume my story.

"Why don't you start from the beginning, Tolliver?"

"Sure. You want me to start from when she first walked into my office, or just what happened tonight?"

"Let's just deal with tonight for the moment."

"Sure thing. About half-an-hour after we talked on the phone, I got a call from Mrs. Mauston. She told me that the police had been here asking questions and she wanted me to come over because she needed my help. I said I would. I called Homicide after that, but you were out, so I left a message."

"That much I know, go on," Miller said impatiently.

"Well, when I got here Mrs. Mauston was in a tizzy. We talked for awhile. She was still pretending that she was innocent, but then she tried to convince me that it would be in both of our best interests if I could kind of persuade the cops that Lomax must have been the one who killed her husband."

"Your best interests, eh?" Miller said with a leer. "What did she mean by that?"

"She promised me a cut of the insurance money. We dickered over that for a bit. She offered me twenty thousand. I was holding out for fifty grand with ten thousand up front."

"You were, were you?"

"I didn't mean it, of course, but I was playing for time, waiting for you to come charging in on a white horse."

"Yeah, I bet. What happened next?"

"Well, we talked it over, then I refused her offer. That's when she pulled that pistol out of the sideboard, the one lying on the floor. I admit that took me by surprise."

"I bet. I wish I had been here to see the look on your face."

"If you had been here, it wouldn't have happened."

"Go on."

"Well, Ada over there relieved me of my gun. By the way, I'm pretty sure she's the one that slugged me the other night as I was leaving here."

"Slugged by a lady's maid, Jim. That will sure help your reputation," Miller commented with a smirk.

"Don't sell her short. She's one of them Midwestern farm girls. Probably grew up carrying cows out to pasture or whatever it is they do in Minnesota. Besides that, she was the one that drove Mrs. Mauston around the night she killed her husband. I'm pretty sure she knew what was going on. I don't know if that makes her an accessory or not. I'll leave that up to the D.A."

"That's mighty generous of you, Tolliver. So she confessed?"

"I wouldn't call it so much a confession as a bragging session, but yeah she said she did it."

"We can talk about that later. Go on with what happened tonight."

"It was about that time that Lomax burst in with a gun in his hand to complete the party. There were some recriminations on both sides, Lomax claiming that he'd been played for a patsy, and Mrs. Mauston telling him that he wasn't half the man her husband had been and that she'd only been using him. For a bit there I thought Lomax might shoot her, but he didn't."

"So if Lomax had the gun, how did he end up being the one that got shot?"

"When Lomax burst in, Mrs. Mauston still had the pistol in her hand. It was kind of a stand-off. As he was getting up the nerve to shoot, she shot first. I managed to knock him out of the way so that he only got winged."

"So you were at least good for something, eh?"

"Yeah. In the confusion, I came up with Lomax's gun. I told her to put hers down. After that, there was some more talking. Helen wanted me to finish Lomax off. She still thought that we could pin the whole business on Lomax, and with him dead, he wouldn't be around to contradict whatever we said. She said that we could go away somewhere together and split the insurance money between us."

"So you'd get the money and the dame?"

"Something like that. I refused, of course. I called the Hall of Justice again asking for an ambulance for Lomax. It wasn't too long after that that you showed up. When I heard you thumping on the door, I must have gotten distracted, because the next thing I know she's got the pistol in her hand and is threatening to kill me because I'd ruined all of her plans. She was going to shoot me, so I shot first. That's when the door came crashing down. The rest you pretty much know firsthand."

"An interesting story, Tolliver. You should write it up for one of them pulp magazines. The question is, how much of it is true?"

"All of it. You can ask Lomax about the parts that he witnessed. You can ask the maid, too, but I'm not sure how much she'll cooperate. It seems she'll do just about anything for Mrs. Mauston."

About that time the fingerprint and crime scene guys showed up pushing Miller and me out of the way while they did their work.

To get out of the way Miller and I moved off into the room that Mr. Mauston had used as his study. Miller planted himself in the chair behind Mauston's desk and helped himself to a cigar from the box that sat in the corner of the desk. I guess he figured Mauston wasn't going to be needing them anymore. He shoved the box in my direction, but I shook my head. I'd never been much for smoking stogies. Instead, I plopped myself into the leather armchair.

"Okay, Jim," Miller resumed. "Say things went down tonight as you said they did, and, mind you, I'm not saying I doubt that. Your shooting Mrs. Mauston will probably be ruled self-defense. That still leaves me with a murder case on my hands. It's not clear that she'll be in any shape to give us a statement anytime soon if ever. Now it sounds like Mrs. Mauston told you what happened that night. Why don't you tell me what *you* think occurred."

"Sure. It was pretty clever when you come down to it. It probably started when Mr. Mauston started thinking about getting a divorce. If he did, there was a good chance that Mrs. Mauston wouldn't get much if anything in the settlement. Mauston had already hired one private investigator to check her out, Lance Donavan."

Miller raised an eyebrow. "Donavan?"

"Yeah. Anyway, the threat of a divorce may have been the reason Mrs. Mauston contemplated murder, though she may have just gotten tired of having a husband and the idea of a quarter of a million became more appealing. Whatever the case, she started to plan the whole thing out.

"The first part of the plan was starting an affair with Lomax, who was just foolish enough to bite. She waited until he was out of town, and then picked a night when her husband would be working late. Evidently, he'd been doing that a lot recently. She wires Lomax that they had a chance to meet and they arrange a tete-a-tete at the Hotel Alexandria. Lomax would take a train in from Salt Lake City and book a room under a fake name and then take the night train back there after they were done. He'd then return to San Francisco on the next night's sleeper."

"I don't get that whole business, Tolliver. Why go to all that trouble?"

"That was done to set up Lomax as the fall guy in case things went wrong. When questioned, he'd tell the police that he'd been in Salt Lake City the whole time to protect Mrs. Mauston's reputation. If his alibi broke down later, then he'd look like the obvious suspect because he had lied to the police. His motive would be that he'd end up owning all the import business due to a clause in the partnership agreement."

"It still seems too complex to me," Miller objected.

"It probably was," I agreed. "Lomax checks into the hotel using the alias Edgar Larkin, and they go up to his room. Sometime after ten, Mrs. Mauston leaves the hotel and is picked up by Ada, her maid in her car. The maid drives Mrs. Mauston to her home where Mrs. Mauston picks up the pistol Mr. Mauston bought her, and then they drive to the office. While in the hotel, she had picked Lomax's pocket and gotten his key to the office, so she unlocks the front door, walks up to the office, surprises Mauston at his desk and shoots him with her own gun which she leaves on the desk as if it had dropped out of Mauston's own hand."

"That seems pretty strange, using your own gun."

"Actually, that was one of the more clever parts of the scheme. The police would think no one would be stupid enough to use their own gun to commit a murder, and it was a gun that Mr. Mauston would have had ready access to. There was no reason to suspect that he hadn't taken it from his wife's drawer and used it to commit suicide. You didn't suspect her initially, did you?"

"No, I guess not," Miller agreed grudgingly.

"After she had shot him, she went down to where Ada was waiting in the car, and she was driven home. When the police came to question her, she said that she'd been home all night. The maid backed up her story. She had an alibi and Lomax had an alibi, even if both were faked. The D.A bought it as a suicide. That might have been the end of the matter, and she would have gotten away with it. Except that she made two mistakes."

"And those were?"

"The first one was that she hadn't read the insurance policy, so she didn't know that they didn't pay out in a case of suicide. That meant that she had to hire a private detective to go stir things up so that Mauston's death would be ruled a homicide."

"You said two mistakes. What was the other?"

"She hadn't counted on Lomax having dinner."

"I don't get it," Miller said.

"When she hired me, Mrs. Mauston let slip the fact that a 'friend' had seen Lomax at the Hotel Alexandria that night. The idea was that I'd poke holes in his alibi and then he'd become the number one suspect. And that's what I did. I went to the hotel and showed the desk clerk Lomax's photo. He recognized it as 'Edgar Larkin.' When I talked to the sleeping car attendant, he remembered that he'd seen Lomax the train the night before going from San Francisco to Salt Lake. That pretty much broke Lomax's alibi."

"Yeah, you told me all that. But what has his having dinner have to do with it?"

"While I was at the hotel, I talked to the maitre d' at the restaurant. He recognized Lomax as having had dinner that night. At ten-thirty. But if Lomax had dinner at ten-thirty and was on a train that left the station in Oakland a little after midnight, he wouldn't have had time to kill Mauston. He'd barely have had enough time to take the ferry and make the train. That pretty much ruled out Lomax as the killer, and that left only one real suspect, Mrs. Mauston."

"Yeah. I see it now. Pretty slick the way you figured it out, Tolliver."

"But not slick enough. Mrs. Mauston hired me, thinking I was just another bumbling private dick, except I wasn't."

"There's one question I've got, though," Miller said.

"What's that?"

"Did you ever feel tempted. I mean, a share of two-hundred fifty G's and a good looking woman like Mrs. Mauston. A lot of guys would have thought about it."

I took a second to answer. "Okay, yeah I thought about it, maybe. But I also thought about the fact that she had killed her husband and double-crossed her lover. Not exactly a great track record is it?"

"No, I guess not," Miller replied.

27.

As I said at the beginning of this yarn, like all good detective stories, this one ends badly for almost everyone involved.

Mrs. Mauston survived being shot, though from what I've heard it was touch and go for awhile. When the case went to trial a couple of months later, the press had a field day with it while it lasted, which wasn't long. By then, the prosecution had sewed up most of the loose ends, and there wasn't much of a defense possible. The jury was out for less than an hour. She was found guilty of first-degree murder and is serving a life sentence.

Ada had been the star witness for the prosecution. She'd turned state's evidence for a reduced charge, and only did six months. They never bothered to charge her for trying to bash my head in. I guess that didn't matter to anyone except me. Last I heard she had moved up to Oregon or Washington State or someplace.

Lomax recovered, more or less, though his left arm doesn't work as well as it used to. The whole business had taken a lot out of him, and he is no longer the suave lady killer that he had once fancied himself. When he had been up on the witness stand during the trial, he'd looked like a beaten man. Afterward, he had thanked me for saving his life, but I hadn't been sure that he'd meant it. When it was all over, he sold Far Eastern, both the store and the import business. He told me that he was going to take the money and try and start over someplace else like Cuba or Panama. I'd wished him luck.

His selling Far Eastern left Miss Bouchet out of a job. I'd offered to take her on as a secretary, but we both knew that I couldn't really afford that. I've met her for dinner several times, which has been pleasant for both of us. Last time I'd talked to her she'd taken a job with an import-export bank where her knowledge of languages will come in handy. I hope she'll do all right for herself.

Officially, Lt. Miller was given credit for solving the Mauston murder. The newspapers had a different idea, operating on the theory that congratulating the police on a job well done doesn't sell nearly as many papers as calling them out for being bumbling incompetents. Depending on the paper, they either castigated Miller for calling Mauston's death a suicide or complained that he had persecuted an innocent man in Lomax. The lieutenant, like the good cop he is, just let the criticism roll off his back.

The only ones who came out of the affair happy were Mandelbrot and the Western National Insurance Company. With Mrs. Mauston convicted of murder, Western National saved themselves two-hundred and fifty thousand dollars. I don't know for sure what Mandelbrot got out of it, but I suspect it was a nice healthy bonus. After about six months a check from Western National showed up in my mailbox. It was for twenty-five hundred dollars, one percent of what I'd saved them. I cashed it anyway.

As for me, well, I got a lump on the head. I got that and the five C-notes that Mrs. Mauston had paid me initially. Minus expenses, of course. I never bothered to file an expense report, and she never complained. What with ferry tickets, taxi fares, car rental, and assorted payments I came out about three-fifty ahead. Not a fortune, but it paid the rent for a while.

I've taken Lt. Miller's advice, and have written the whole story down just as it happened for the pulps. I don't know if it will ever see print, but you never know.

AN AUTHOR'S ADMISSION

The San Francisco depicted in *Murder After Midnight* is a product of my imagination. I've never lived in the city, though I've visited it on a number of occasions. More importantly, I wasn't there in the 1930s when the novel is set. I have spent time in the Bay area including several months in Olema, but the city portrayed in this book owes more to the Continental Op stories of Dashiell Hammett and his famous novel *The Maltese Falcon*, as well as lesser-known works such as Fritz Lieber's *Our Lady of Darkness* and Dorothy Bennett's *Murder Unleased*, than it does to reality.

I have tried to be as true to the actual geography as much as possible based on maps and my memories. I've also drawn on a number of books for inspiration and information, in particular, Don Herron's delightful *The Dashiell Hammett Tour*. Some locations are real places, though a few are under aliases, and some are just plain made up. Any errors, inaccuracies, or inconsistencies are my own fault and should not be blamed on anyone else.

As far as Olema goes, I did live there for several months in the 1970s, and the descriptions are drawn from that time. I don't think it was much different then than it had been in the 1930s. It certainly hadn't changed much when I revisited it a few years ago.

Why set a mystery novel in 1930s San Francisco, a city I've never lived in, and in a time from before I was born? The answer is simple; San Francisco is a city made for detective stories, and the 1930s is the perfect period for the type of story I wanted to write. I'm not the first writer to feel that way, and I'm pretty sure I won't be the last.

I hope you enjoy this book despite this admission.

Greg Fowlkes
June, 2018

SPECIAL PREVIEW!

A FICTIONAL DETECTIVE TRIFECTA

~ NOVELLAS FEATURING
THE FICTIONAL DETECTIVE ~

Now available from The Fictional Press
www.TheFictionalPress.com

FROM THE WIZARD AT LAW SERIES BY GREG FOWLKES

THE LAWS OF MAGIC

Egil Njalsson was an aspiring lawyer. A lawyer with a difference. Not only had he passed the bar, but he had an undergraduate degree from the most prestigious school of magic in the country, the California Institute of Thaumaturgy. Needless to say, his caseload and clients tended to the unusual. Like witches; or vampires. And the opposition, well they were likely to be demons. But Egil Njalsson had sworn an oath to uphold the law of the land, and... *The Laws of Magic*!

TRIAL BY MAGIC

Egil Njalsson is just another practicing attorney. Except, that is, for the occasional unusual client. Such as the ghost who retained his services using e-mail. Or the wolf who has been cursed by an Indian shaman to turn into a human during the full moon. Or the Leprechaun who is facing the loss of his saloon. Even when the clients are human, they have unusual problems like the Creole chef accused of making a rival a zombie or the scientist accused of transmuting a man into a statue of silicon. Yet somehow, Egil manages to resolve all his client's problems whether legal or magical. Of course, it helps that he is a wizard as well as a lawyer.

Trial by Magic includes five new tales from the same world as *The Laws of Magic*.

FROM THE MURDER ON MARS SERIES BY GREG FOWLKES

BLOOD REDS SANDS OF MARS

On Mars, the wind was rising. The grains of sand could be heard abrading the thin aluminum skin that was the only protection against the outside. On the far side of Olympus Mons, a prospector lies dead in the sand. Inspector Erik McKernan, head of the handful of men that make up the small Martian police force must find the killer while threading the maze of corporate and international politics that govern the planet, and he must do it while trying to survive . . .*The Blood Red Sands of Mars!*

A DEATH AT STATION ALPHA

Station Alpha, a remote Martian research facility isolated by a planet-wide dust storm. When one of the scientists is found murdered, it falls to Inspector McKernan to determine which of the remaining twelve people at the station wielded the fatal weapon. But, as the crime was committed in a locked laboratory with no possible access and all the suspects would seem to have unbreakable alibis, it will take all his skills as a detective to solve the puzzle of *A Death at Station Alpha.* Thirty years in the making, the long-awaited sequel to *The Blood Red Sands of Mars.*

A Corpse in Hut Town

Hut Town is the remnants of the original Martian settlement; a collection of inflatable buildings abandoned by the Trust Authority and the mining corporations and now occupied by those catering to the baser needs of miners and construction workers in for a spree. But when a corpse is found in one of the service tunnels, Chief Inspector McKernan is called in.

He has plenty of questions. Who's body is it? How did they die? How did they get to Mars in the first place, and why weren't they missed? And the most important one on the Inspector's mind— are there any more bodies down there?

Murder at the Mars Club

The Mars Club was the sanctuary of the rich and powerful on Mars, so when one of the members is found dead, Chief Inspector is called in to solve the case as discretely as possible. Will the solution of the case prove to be the one man he'd least like to implicate?

FROM THE FICTIONAL DETECTIVE SERIES BY GREG FOWLKES

THE FICTIONAL DETECTIVE

Mystery writer Ezekial O. Handler has been killed in a suspicious car crash. Private detective Frank Slade has been hired by Handler's beautiful girlfriend to investigate. Handler, seemingly with a premonition of his death, has left a trail of clues. Can Slade discover the murderer, or will he instead uncover a secret that will shake his existence to the core?

A FICTIONAL DETECTIVE TRIFECTA

The Fictional Detective has gotten out of the Private Investigator game. Instead, he's trying to write hard-boiled masterpieces such as *Death Buys a Condo*. But despite the fact that the door of his office now says WRITER, some of his clients haven't gotten the word. And a strange lot of clients they are. A man that only contacts him during séances because, well, he's dead; a female impersonator who has inherited a house that's just a little too haunted for the market, and a small-time gambler who's trying to end an affair with Lady Luck.

Three All New Novellas featuring the Fictional Detective!

The Fictional Press
www.TheFictionalPress.com

The Fictional Press is a small, independent press specializing in the publication of fictional works by emerging authors. If you are interested in bringing your fictional works to life in print as well as electronically, contact us! We can help!

Find out more at www.thefictionalpress.com.